SHADOW WAR

SHADOWS OF THE VOID BOOK 10

J.J. GREEN

INFINITEBOOK

BOOKS ORDER

The Books of Shadows of the Void - Complete Series

Prequel: Starbound

Book 1: Generation

Book 2: Stranded

Book 3: Dawn

Book 4: Shadowrise

Book 5: Underworld

Book 6: Burned

Book 7: Trapped

Book 8: Mars Born

Book 9: Shadow Battle

Book 10: Shadow War

Books 1 - 3 The Galathea Chronicles

Books 4 - 7 The Earth Chronicles

Books 8 - 10 The Galactic Chronicles

1

———

The destroyer *Thylacine* materialized from a starjump, and Commander Jas Harrington immediately leaned forward in her seat. A hologram blinked into life in front of her—a golden globe slowly spinning in mid-air, filling one-fifth of the *Thylacine's* bridge. A dry, cloudless planet.

The planet's name was unpronounceable in English, but that didn't matter. It was one of several worlds that was home to a rich source of mythrin, the raw ingredient of the stupor-inducing, extraordinarily expensive, highly illegal drug, mythranil. As such, the world was extremely likely to have been infiltrated by the hostile aliens known as Shadows.

Infiltrated, and secured.

The Shadows aimed to cut off the Unity Alliance's supply of mythranil so the UA's Shadow scanners wouldn't work and their ability to tell friend from foe would be lost.

"Force field maximum power," said First Officer Trimborn. "Scanning for enemy ships."

Jas nodded. Everyone aboard knew the drill. If the battle scenario played out as it usually did, they had about five seconds.

Four. Three. Two—

"Pulses incoming," exclaimed Trimborn.

The Shadow ship protecting the planet had spotted them and fired.

"Got the origin coordinates," said another officer. "Returning fire."

Vibrations shook Jas's seat and the arm rests beneath her hands. The enemy's pulses had hit the ship, but the *Thylacine's* force field was strong. They had plenty of power, enough for a long, pitched battle. The trick to winning was to destroy the opposition before the power ran out.

"Picking up the Shadow ship," said Trimborn, looking from his screen to the holo. A starship appeared over the edge of the golden globe. Long, slim, and sprouting four curved extensions, the ship was a make that Jas didn't recognize. Like most Shadow ships, it had probably been built by the native population on the planet below and stolen by the aliens after their invasion.

The *Thylacine's* pulses were already streaming toward it.

"Fire again," Jas said. "Full attack."

"Yes, Commander."

"Halve our distance from that ship, Pilot," said Jas.

Pilot Kennewell replied, "Engaging Raptors, ma'am."

Acceleration from the propulsion engines pushed Jas back in her seat as the *Thylacine* sped toward its attacker, following the barrage of pulses it had launched. A similar assault from the Shadow ship clashed into the *Thylacine's* pulses. The bolts of raw energy collided, exploded, and dispersed in the high thermosphere above the planet. The *Thylacine* continued full speed ahead, cutting through the cloud of energized particles, leaving behind a charged wake. Jas hoped the battle was visible to the population below, giving the invasion survivors the news that the Unity Alliance had come to their rescue.

"A second ship's jumped in," exclaimed Trimborn.

The hologram echoed his words. Before the first officer had finished speaking, another starship winked into existence. It appeared directly behind the *Thylacine*, so close that the energy of its starjump hit them full force, rocking the ship.

"Krat," muttered Jas, gripping her armrests to steady herself. There was no way the Shadows could have messaged for reinforcements. The *Thylacine* was dampening their comms. She was confident of that. This was bad luck—a pure coincidence that her destroyer had happened to arrive moments before a second Shadow ship. It was probably there to relieve the first or was intended to double the planet's defenses.

This battle wasn't going to be as straightforward as Jas had hoped. "Fire away at our second target."

"Already on it, ma'am," came the reply. The pulses flew out toward the new aggressor.

The officer should have awaited her order, but she didn't object. Her team were battle-seasoned. She trusted them to use their initiative, and they knew it. The new ship would take about a second to activate its force field post-jump. If the *Thylacine* could score a hit during that time window, it would do significant damage. Waiting for her command would only have wasted precious time.

"Direct hit," said the officer.

The *Thylacine* continued to zoom closer to the original Shadow ship and away from their surprise attacker. The ship they were leaving behind shuddered as their pulses hit it. Jas craned forward, looking expectantly at the ship. They had to have hit it before its force field was full power, but the holo displayed no debris.

"We didn't breech her hull," exclaimed Trimborn.

"Maintain fire," Jas said evenly, settling backward into her seat. "Equal pulses. Both ships." They were now under attack from two directions.

She bit the edge of her thumb. Failure to inflict serious damage when a ship's force field was down was rare. She peered at the new ship. It was another kind that she'd never seen before. In five years of battles, Jas had seen many starships fighting on both sides of the Shadow War. She'd gotten to know most of the models and their specs and capabilities. Only occasionally now did she encounter an unfamiliar ship. Yet here were two that she didn't know. She wondered if the Shadows had begun to design and manufacture their own ships.

The second ship began its pursuit. The *Thylacine* continued on its course, closing the distance with the first ship. They were fast becoming penned in. Jas clenched her jaw. Taking out one average Shadow ship was achievable. The *Thylacine* had done it often enough. Taking out two— one of which seemed exceptionally well-protected—would be tough.

"Pulses incoming," Trimborn said. They were too numerous for the *Thylacine's* pulses to intercept.

The ship vibrated again under the heavy fire.

"Fighters launched from Shadow Ship Two," said Trimborn. Sparks spewed from the side of the second ship, the tiny flecks of light representing manned Shadow fighter ships.

Jas's stomach twisted at the sight. She raised her comm

button to her lips. "Squadron Leader Correia, scramble all fighters."

She imagined the Unity Alliance fighter pilots in their single-seater, highly maneuverable ships as they bravely prepared to launch. Starship force fields protected them against high-energy pulses, but close-range, low-energy fighter fire could penetrate the defensive screen. Protracted fighter fire on vulnerable spots could cripple a ship. The *Thylacine's* fighter pilots would protect against these attacks and attempt to destroy the enemy's fighters.

Despite the danger to her ship from the Shadow fighter attack, Jas hated deploying her pilots. Their chances of survival were terrible. In the average Shadow War battle, fewer than sixty percent of UA pilots would make it back to their ships alive. Jas's pilot survival stats were somewhat better, mostly because she did whatever she could to avoid risking her pilots' lives. It was something Admiral Pacheco criticized her for, though she'd never lost a battle yet.

In the current situation, however, she had no choice.

"Kennewell," she said. "As the last fighter leaves, take us hard to port." The *Thylacine's* fighter ships would launch to starboard. She needed to give the pilots room to maneuver, and she wanted to avoid becoming sandwiched between the two Shadow ships.

"Yes, ma'am," Kennewell replied, her hands hovering over her controls.

The ship continued to vibrate as the odd attacking pulse impacted their force field. Their own pulses were also scoring hits, too, gradually wearing down their enemies' power levels.

Inertia pushed Jas to the right as Kennewell swiftly maneuvered the ship. The *Thylacine's* fighters were now visible on the holo, specks of light swirling around, streaming out to meet the enemy's oncoming ships.

"Drop force field power fifty percent. Divert to pulses. Direct all pulse fire at ship one," Jas commanded, judging that the second ship wouldn't fire through the ranks of their own fighters to attack the *Thylacine*. Temporarily diverting her ship's force field power to pulses was worth the risk. They had to hit the first ship with everything they had.

The *Thylacine's* bolts poured across space toward the first Shadow ship. The pulses the destroyer emitted were so intense they looked like one long chain of light leading from the *Thylacine* to its enemy. They swamped the enemy ship with energy.

Trimborn was intent on his scanner. "Their force field's breaking down, Commander."

"Fighter fire at our launch bay doors," another officer said.

Jas's gaze swept the interplay of fighter ships. They were executing a macabre dance in the space between the *Thylacine* and the second Shadow ship. Some enemy fighters had slipped through her pilots' defenses, and sprays of flickering sparks were springing out and onto the *Thylacine*. Her fighters had spotted the attack, however. Several peeled away from the rest and swept back toward the ship.

"We're through," exclaimed Trimborn.

Jas clicked her tongue. Her first officer's speech always became vague when he was over-excited. "We've broken through ship one's force field, Trimborn?"

"Yes, ma'am. Sorry, ma'am."

Then the bridge of the *Thylacine* shook so violently, Jas was almost thrown from her seat. "Force field one hundred percent," she barked as she recovered her balance. "Damage report."

"They've blasted our bay doors wide open," an officer said. "But—"

Trimborn gave a whoop. "We've got them!"

Jas turned to the holo to see if Trimborn meant what she thought he meant. Sure enough, the first Shadow ship's curved extensions on one side had been blown clean off and were spinning away into space. As she watched, another of the *Thylacine's* pulses hit the ship, cleaving the central section in half.

"The Shadow fighters are returning to ship two," said an officer.

As if in response to the first ship's destruction, the specks of light from the second ship were speeding home. Jas frowned. The fighter ships had succeeded in hitting the *Thylacine*. Why were they giving up their attack? Their actions could mean only one thing, Jas realized. But surely it was too soon for that?

As the enemy fighters left the battle scene, the *Thylacine's* did the same, clearing the path for pulses. Not for the first time, Jas was grateful for her smart squadron leader. Once the fighters were outside the ship, both sides' comm dampeners made giving orders impossible. The pilots were trained in set responses to certain events during an engagement.

"Ship two's building energy," Trimborn said.

"Fire at will," commanded Jas. They would make the best use of the remaining time.

Now that the pathway was clear, the *Thylacine* poured pulses onto the enemy ship. But their attack seemed to have little impact. Like its hull, the ship's force field was formidable.

The *Thylacine's* pulses were bathing the enemy ship in light, so that only its outline was visible above the slowly turning golden globe. Everyone on the bridge fixed their gaze on the starship. No one even seemed to breathe.

Then it was gone.

There was a sigh of exhaled breath. The second ship had jumped. Relieved exclamations sounded across the bridge.

"I want a full damage report," Jas barked. "Begin repairs immediately, and scan the remaining ship's debris for signs of life. Trimborn, assemble a team to sweep the planet."

Her tone quietened the room, and heads turned to consoles as everyone went back to their tasks.

Jas frowned. The battle had been much too easy. Why hadn't the second ship stuck around? Her fighters had penetrated the *Thylacine's* defenses, and expended power made the ship additionally vulnerable.

The two new models of starships added to Jas's suspicions. She would have to speak to Pacheco the next opportunity she had.

Her expression turned grim. Her next task was a sad one. After briefly checking that everyone on the bridge was focused on their work, she opened the interface on her armrest.

The screen displayed a list of pilots' names. As the fighter pilots returned to the ship, their embedded microchips would be recognized by the ship's computer. A dot would appear next to each name as the pilots landed. The search for missing pilots would begin immediately. When it was completed, Jas would write to the families of those who hadn't been found. She would tell them that their loved one was missing in action, presumed dead.

Pacheco had told her several times that she didn't have to do this task, but she did it anyway. The reason was, each time that she did it, she was reminded of a pilot she had once known.

Jas performed this service for missing pilots' families because she knew that *she* would have liked to have received that news rather than being left never really knowing what had happened to him.

2

____

Jas's office was bare and functional. She had a desk with an embedded interface and a seat. A couple more chairs stood against the wall in case she ever felt the need to invite anyone to sit, but the seats were rarely used. She wasn't a commander who was in the habit of having long conversations with her crew.

With a sigh, she swept the screen of her interface, and it blinked to life. The damage report from the battle was in. She scanned it, her tired gaze moving down the screen. The *Thylacine* had sustained severe damage to the launch bay doors, but repair crews were already working on them. The area would be without an atmosphere until the doors were fixed.

She had sent First Officer Trimborn planetside to sweep the population for Shadows. He and his defense units and troops would work through the government and other positions of influence in the local population, employing Shadow scanners to root out the aliens. Control of the planet would be returned to its sentient species, and Trimborn's team would train key personnel in the Transgalactic

Council's Shadow protocol: rigorous, systematic testing for the Shadows' presence in every area of their society.

How the locals dealt with the Shadows they discovered was up to them, providing they ensured the hostile aliens would no longer pose any threat to the galaxy. In Jas's experience, most of the invaded populations chose to put an end to that threat once and for all.

Some armed resistance during the Shadow sweeping process was almost inevitable, but Trimborn had troops, weapons, and armored vehicles. The fighter ships could also operate in an atmosphere if needed. Trimborn was well-practiced at his task, and Jas had every confidence in her first officer, even if he was prone to getting a little over-excited at times.

As she finished reading the damage report, she frowned. The enhanced capabilities of the Shadow ship and its fighter pilots, and its surprise retreat, still bothered her. With a sinking heart, she pulled up the list of pilots. Where there should have been dots, many blanks remained next to the names. She lifted her comm button to her lips.

"Squadron Leader Correia, report on the missing pilots."

"We've finished our search, ma'am. Everyone who's coming back is aboard ship," came the man's reply.

Krat. The list on the display looked more than half empty. "We seem to have suffered higher than average losses."

"Yes, we have, Commander. Thirty-three missing."

Thirty-three of seventy-eight. "How do you account for those numbers, Squadron Leader?"

The man took a moment to answer. "If I'm honest, Commander, I'd say we were outclassed. If it weren't for the fact that the second ship jumped, I don't think we could have lasted much longer."

"I see."

"I've been a part of this war for nearly three years, ma'am," Correia went on, "and the Shadow fighter pilots just get better and better. At the same time, our recruits are younger every time we receive a new batch, and they're worse-trained. When I joined up, I thought the caliber of our pilots was poor and we were scraping the barrel. Now, if it weren't for the fact that we've got a war to win, I would send half of every new intake back to pilot school." The man's tone rose. "They simply aren't ready, ma'am. And we send them out there like... like... "

"I understand, Squadron Leader," Jas said. "I understand. Please let me know when we'll hold the memorial service for the lost pilots."

Correia had recovered his composure. He answered firmly, "Yes, ma'am."

Jas closed the comm link and returned her attention to the screen. She prepared to write the first mail of thirty-three. Pressing on a pilot's name brought up his or her details, including the next-of-kin's mail address and any last messages or requests from the pilot in the event of their death. She always read each entry carefully and crafted personal mails based on what the pilot had written. She pressed the first name:

If I don't make it, please send this message to my parents:

Dear Mom and Dad, don't cry too long or too hard over me. Please don't be mad over what has happened. I did what I had to do, and fighting the Shadows was it. Put on a brave face for those who need you, and celebrate my life.

Jas read the woman's birth date. She'd been twenty-two when she died. Her eyes sad, Jas began to write.

She always referred to the lost pilot's status as 'presumed dead'. If the searchers couldn't find a signal from their chip, the person was almost certainly going to die if they weren't already dead. Deep space was so vast, the chances of being accidentally found were just about impossible. Though Jas recalled a case where the pilot's arm that held her chip had been blown way off into space, and it was only when she managed to comm her ship that anyone knew she was still alive.

Jas had only written two sentences of the first mail when her interface chirruped. The message wasn't marked urgent, so she ignored it. Whatever it was, it could wait until she'd gotten at least one mail written. Almost immediately, however, there was a second chirrup. This time, she checked to see who was messaging her. It was Admiral Pacheco's office requesting a vidcall.

She rolled her eyes. Vidcalls across space required excessive power. A simple mail should have sufficed if he wanted to discuss something, and whatever it was could probably have been handled by his office too.

She pressed her acceptance, and Pacheco's familiar face appeared on her screen. She'd worked with him in one way or another ever since she had volunteered to join the Shadow War and he was first officer aboard the *Infineon*, where she'd been posted. Jas had been commanding a team of defense units, and Pacheco had earned a quick promotion to commander when the *Infineon's* commander had his head blown off by a Shadow.

Jas and Pacheco had both come a long way since then, and the admiral's dark hair had silvered at his temples. Over the years, Jas had developed a comfortable acquaintance with the short-tempered man.

If only the admiral's feelings about her had been similarly neutral.

"Commander Harrington, good to see you, as always."

"Hello, Admiral. Is there something I can do for you?"

The man's features clouded. "Ever efficient and straight to the point. Would it hurt to just chat for once, Jas? It isn't like we're strangers."

She rubbed her brow. "I'm in the middle of something, Pacheco. So, if this is about the meeting, don't worry, I haven't forgotten. Now, I really need to—"

"You're writing to the pilots' families, aren't you? I keep telling you—"

"And I keep telling *you* that I want to do it. Now, please, krat knows how much power this call is using, so..."

"Okay, okay," the admiral grumbled. "Yes, it was about the meeting. But not only that, you'll collect your new intake of personnel while you're here and jump back to your ship with them. You have some newly trained pilots, a team of defense units, a chief engineer, and relief maintenance crew as your current set are at the end of their duty tour, some medics, and—"

"Fine. I'll make sure to collect them. I'll see you at the meeting."

"Wait," Pacheco said. "There's one more thing I thought you might be interested to know."

"What's that?" Jas asked, wondering what else the man would think up to prolong the call. She lifted her hand, ready to close the connection.

"As your intake were talking among themselves, I overheard something I thought you might find interesting. One of them already knows you, someone said. From way back before the Shadow War began."

Jas's hand halted on its downward trajectory to end the call. "Someone who knows me?" Her voice quivered.

Pacheco's eyes narrowed as he studied her reaction. "Yes, that's right. That was all I heard, though."

Someone who knew her. For a brief moment, Jas forgot where she was and who she was talking to. But she didn't dare to hope.

She returned to the present and saw that Pacheco had been watching her silently during her moment of distraction.

"Okay," she said, with some effort. "Thanks for letting me know. I'll see you soon."

She closed the call without waiting for an answer. Her heart was racing and her blood was rushing through her ears, making her light-headed. Could it really be him? It was hardly possible that he'd survived five years as a pilot in the Shadow War. The attrition rate was too high. She hadn't met a single pilot who had been in the war since the beginning.

Her stomach was so tight, she felt sick. It was strange. She thought she'd given up hope of ever seeing Carl again years ago, when she'd accepted the remoteness of the chances of him still being alive. Yet this small remark passed on by Pacheco had thrown her back into a state of ridiculous, stupid hope. A hope she'd tried hard to give up.

3

___

Jas had a few minutes before the Transgalactic Council gateway would open to take her to the Unity Alliance meeting. She checked her reflection in her cabin's mirror, smoothing down the creases on her uniform pants. She preferred the flexibility of a combat suit to the stiff, black material of a commander's uniform. Hers always looked crumpled and untidy.

She had managed to slow her racing heart a little by telling herself over and over again that it was impossible that this person who knew her from long ago could be Carl. She had met and worked with many people over her career as a security officer. Hundreds of crew members aboard the prospecting starships where she used to work, in fact. This person could be any of them. There was no reason for her to suppose that it was Carl.

She checked the time and turned to face the spot in the corner of her office where the gateway would open. The technology was highly confidential. The Council insisted that it was used well away from lower-ranking military.

Minute green specks appeared in midair and were soon

lazily swirling around. Jas had gotten used to traveling by gateway since she'd been promoted to commander six months ago, but she took deep breaths this time as the green spots coalesced.

At just the right moment, she stepped through.

She was in the entrance way of a tall building, standing in the bright light of twin suns. Jas stepped quickly away from the gateway to make room for other commanders and captains who would be appearing behind her. Looking up, she saw that her initial impression of the building hadn't been correct. It would have been more accurate to describe the place as a kind of mound. Way above, the massive insectoid Transgalactic Council officials were flying on translucent wings, emerging from and landing at holes in the sides.

The entrance way she stood at was apparently only for species who went around on legs. Jas took a moment to enjoy the feeling of sunlight on her face for the first time in months before entering the edifice.

Inside, she was greeted by a Council administrator—a smaller, less colorful version of the higher officials—who led her and the other military officers through smooth, ceramic tunnels to the meeting room.

Accommodating the range of galactic species who had allied with the Unity, the military arm of the Transgalactic Council, could not have been easy, but the Council managers had clearly grown adept at the practice during the hundreds of Earth years that they'd been organizing the galaxy's affairs. Jas settled down in a seat designed for humanoids and waited for the rest of the UA officers to arrive.

She'd been eager to attend the meeting after her most recent battle, to discuss what had happened with the new Shadow ships. She'd wanted to find out if anyone had had a similar experience and what they thought of it. But Pacheco's news had distracted her a little. She was looking forward to the meeting being over so she could meet this mysterious person from the past who knew her.

The Unity Alliance officers entered the room in dribs and drabs, walking, hopping, floating, and sliding. Jas knew many of them by sight, some by name. During her brief time as a commander, some of the officers she'd gotten to know had died in the course of performing their duty.

She chewed the edge of her thumb, wondering how much longer she had to wait until the meeting would start.

Finally, when the room was bursting with the assorted UA upper echelons, Admiral Pacheco arrived. As he came in, his eyes caught Jas's. His black uniform was in a far better state than hers. Not a crease or piece of lint was in sight. He was wearing his admiral's hat, which he took off and tucked under his arm.

Only an extra star on the breast of his jacket signified Pacheco's rank, but his dignified composure was enough to tell any onlooker of his status. His gaze, as it swept the room, was quiet and serious. The hum of various languages that had started up as the officers waited was quickly silenced.

"Commanders, captains, rear admirals, thank you for coming," Pacheco said. "Time is pressing, so let's keep this short. I want a brief update from each of you on the recent and ongoing engagements in your sectors."

Jas listened for a moment to the incomprehensible sounds being made by the commander next to Pacheco, who had taken it upon him- or herself to begin, before she realized she'd forgotten to turn her comm button to its translation setting. As soon as she made the change, the button relayed the speech in standard English. The commander was reporting on a successful raid on a Shadow trap planet.

From the description, the world sounded similar to K.67092d, where Jas had first encountered the hostile beings that came from the Void, somewhere outside the known universe. K.67092d had been a barren planet, devoid of complex life forms. Nothing but the strange, hexagonal Shadow traps was of any interest in the place, and that of course made them perfect for attracting the attention of unsuspecting visitors.

The commander related how his crew had successfully destroyed all the traps on the planet. At the same time, they had defended the place from attacking Shadow ships that were seeking to stop them.

The next Unity Alliance officer told a different story. This officer's ship had been tasked with discovering new instances of Shadow invasion that had gone unnoticed by local populations. Galactic civilizations were numerous, and many hadn't yet joined the Transgalactic Council. That fact didn't make them off bounds to the Shadows, however, and to truly remove the Shadow threat from the galaxy, the Council had implemented a program to comb its reaches for their presence.

Not for the first time, Jas was reminded of the Shadows' resemblance to an infestation. Insidious and difficult to permanently eradicate, the aliens had gradually crept into every nook and cranny of the galaxy. They hid away, slowly multiplying, until they finally erupted like a nest of cockroaches.

When Jas's turn came, she told the room about the *Thylacine's* most recent engagement. She emphasized the second Shadow ship's superior fighter pilots, hull, and force field, as well as its puzzling disappearance the minute the first ship was destroyed. When she'd finished her short report, Jas looked to Pacheco for a response, but he gave none. He nodded toward the next officer to begin.

Her brows knitted. Hadn't he understood that there had to be implications to what she'd said? She bit the edge of her thumb again, then stopped because it was already sore.

After what seemed like a long time, the final report was given.

"Thank you, everyone," Pacheco said. "Plenty of useful information there. I also have a report to give. I'm sure you can tell from the many positive stories we've heard here, that the war is going well for us. At the last reckoning, the Unity Alliance effort had eradicated the Shadow threat from approximately ninety-five percent of the galaxy. The scanning protocols the Transgalactic Council put in place two years ago have been working, and the sloppy mistakes we used to make, allowing Shadows to infiltrate the scanning process, are a thing of the past.

"Through the excellent efforts of Commander Harrington and the *Thylacine*—" Jas cringed "—we have secured the Council's access to mythrin, which is of course essential in detecting Shadows. Every day we draw closer to our goal of destroying every known and unknown Shadow invasion." He gave a tight smile. "I think it's safe to say we have the misborns on the run. And now, on to our next maneuver."

Pacheco tapped an interface on the wall. The lights dimmed and a panoply of stars shimmered into view in the center of the room. For a moment, Jas was distracted from her personal concerns. It had been a long time since she'd seen a hologram of the Milky Way. She was used to seeing holos of the local star system wherever the *Thylacine* was engaging in battle. It was only rarely that she saw the galaxy as a whole.

The vast expanse of tiny points of light, representing gigantic, blazing suns, took her breath away.

"Through the efforts of the last five years and the sacrifice of many, many brave individuals," said Pacheco, "we have concentrated the mass of the Shadows in this sector of the galaxy." The holo zoomed into an area of thousands of stars. "According to our intelligence, several star systems in this region remain heavily infested with Shadows. In fact, we're confident that this is where most of the resistance and re-emergences in previously swept sectors are organized and provisioned. It's a Shadow stronghold, but it's the last one. If we can wipe them out here, we have a chance of putting an end to the Shadow menace forever. In short, if we win back this region we will have victory. The war will be over, and the civilizations of the galaxy can return to peace."

Pacheco stopped speaking, but no one said anything for a while. Jas, too, was having trouble processing what the admiral had said. The Shadow War had been going on for so long, fighting it had become a way of life to her. She found it hard to believe that the war *could* end.

A strangled sound, which Jas realized after a moment was a kind of laughter, came from a corner of the room. More sounds and voices joined in, rejoicing at Pacheco's announcement. But before things could get out of hand, the admiral raised his arms and asked for silence.

"Let's not be premature," he said. "We have a lot of work to do before we can celebrate. Now, more than ever, we must continue in our attitude of utmost vigilance to prevent Shadows from infiltrating our safeguards. We must continue to protect our people from their invasions. We must continue to crush and eradicate them wherever we find them.

"I've brought you here today to tell you that we're on the cusp of our best chance for a final, decisive blow. Now, I want you all to return to your ships and redouble your efforts. Expect and accept only the best from those you command. If we can maintain the courage, rigor, and determination that have brought us this far, we can succeed in putting an end to this war. When the time comes for the final push, I will send instructions."

Nothing more needed to be said. The Unity Alliance officers slowly filed out of the room to return to their starships. As Jas had seated herself at the back, she was one of the last to leave. Pacheco was thanking or having brief chats with the officers as they left, but he was alone when Jas reached him.

She tensed.

"Commander Harrington, could I have a word?"

4

———

As always, Pacheco's demeanor lost some of its stiffness now that he and Jas were alone.

"I just wanted to say, congratulations on another successful battle. How many does that make now? Is it eight or nine?"

Jas smiled, thin-lipped. "I've commanded the *Thylacine* for seven battles so far, Admiral."

"Good work. I knew I was making the right decision when I recommended you for promotion."

Jas didn't reply. Was he expecting her to thank him? She'd guessed long ago that Pacheco was at least partly responsible for her rapid rise through the ranks. That and the terrible losses the Unity Alliance had sustained over the years of the war. But the office of commander didn't mean anything to her. She would have served just as conscientiously if she'd been in the lowest ranks. What was more, serving as a commander brought responsibilities that she didn't relish, though she did her best to fulfill them.

The pause was becoming awkward, so Jas said, "I need

to go and find my new intake, sir, and the ship that'll take us to the *Thylacine*."

Pacheco nodded. "Yes, of course. I'll go along with you. It's on my way."

Jas sighed inwardly as they left the room together and entered the labyrinthine tunnels of the Transgalactic Council offices.

"What did you think of the meeting today, Harrington?" Pacheco asked.

"I thought it went well, sir," Jas replied. "I was surprised to hear that we're so close to victory. It feels like we've been fighting this war forever."

"Yes, it feels like that to me too, sometimes," Pacheco said. "Do you mind if I ask, when it's all finally over, what you plan to do?"

"I don't think I have a plan. I've been concentrating on fighting for so long, it's hard to think about the future."

"Will you return to Earth, do you think? Or maybe another planet?"

Earth? Jas hadn't thought about Earth in a long while, and when she did, she usually thought of her old friend, Sayen, ex-navigator of the prospecting starship *Galathea*. She hadn't been able to contact Sayen after they'd both volunteered, due to the security ban on personal comms. She had no idea where she was or even if she was still alive. But she knew that if Sayen survived, *she* would be returning to Earth. Her brother and the woman she loved were there. As to where Jas would go when they finally defeated the Shadows...

"I've no idea," she answered.

They went through a round doorway. Pacheco had brought her to a large waiting area where a group of people and defense units were milling about. It was the usual ragtag bunch. Half already in uniform, half in civvies. Some faces were lined and harried, others looked as though they shouldn't have been let out of school. The defense units were a range of models too. Commandeered from private companies, most likely, or judging from the appearance of some of them, snatched at the last minute from conveyor belts at recycling plants.

Jas's heart began to race as she scanned the faces that turned toward her and Pacheco, but after a few moments, it abruptly slowed and was heavy in her chest. In spite of the five years that had passed, she knew she would notice Carl immediately if he were there. He wasn't.

She realized that the group were saluting her and the admiral. She returned the salute, and from the corner of her eye she noticed Pacheco's gaze upon her while he also saluted. Had he been observing her reaction to seeing the new recruits?

"Thank you. I'll take over from here," she said.

"Yes, Commander. Your transport is waiting on the pad. Safe journey."

"Thank you."

Usually, she was tolerant toward the man's unwanted attention, but her sense of disappointment at not finding Carl among the crowd had irritated her. As the admiral left, she went after him into the empty corridor where she could not be overheard. She said, "Pacheco." He turned, and she went on, "In the meeting, you singled me out for praise. Please don't do that. It's embarrassing."

Pacheco raised his eyebrows and gave a slight shake of his head before walking away.

Jas returned to the room and the waiting women, men, and defense units, already regretting her inappropriate words to the admiral. The man couldn't help his feelings for her any more than she could help the fact that she didn't reciprocate them.

"Who's the highest-ranking person here?" she asked.

A man raised his hand and opened his mouth to speak.

Jas interrupted, "Great. Get everyone onto the transport waiting for us on the launch pad in five minutes."

"Yes, Commander," the man replied.

Jas left to make her own way to the launch pad, guessing that the warren of Council offices had to offer a different route. She wanted to be alone and compose herself before joining the new recruits. She didn't trust herself to maintain a calm attitude in her current state.

She was surprised the disappointment of not finding Carl among the new intake had hit her so hard. It seemed her heart hadn't listened to her head saying time and time again he had to have died.

Her circuitous route brought her to the transport a few minutes after the new crew members of the *Thylacine*. The man who had led them had done a good job. Their packs were safely stowed and everyone was strapped into jumpseats in the bare, functional military transport cabin. All they were waiting for before starjumping was her.

She gave a brief, approving nod before strapping herself in and comm'ing the pilot that they were ready for liftoff. From behind came the soft whoosh and click of the cabin doors shutting automatically, and the rumble of the engines shook her seat.

As the transport rose, wobbling a little, into the air, a realization niggled at Jas. Pacheco's tip had led her to a doomed hope that she might see Carl. When she hadn't, she'd lost interest in the question of who the person from her past might be.

The transport forced its way upward through the

atmosphere and against the pull of gravity. Jas was sitting at the front of the cabin near the door to the cockpit. She craned her head around her seat while the transport rose higher, but all she could see were a few recruits sitting in the row behind her. They returned her gaze with puzzled expressions.

She quickly straightened up. A commander had to maintain a level of dignity, which was one of the things she hated about the position.

There were no windows in the transport, but long experience told Jas they had to be leaving the planet's atmosphere by that time. If she could look out, she would have seen the curve of the globe and the dark expanse of space above.

The transport completed the remainder of its flight away from the planet to a distance from which it would be safe to starjump. Jas racked her brains to match her brief glimpse of a faintly familiar face with a memory of a past acquaintance.

It wasn't until they jumped she had the answer.

5

———

She had never quite gotten used to the rough military transport starjumps. Her stomach lurched as they reappeared in space some distance from the *Thylacine.* The destroyer was still orbiting the mythrin-harboring planet. Whenever she returned to the ship from a trip away, Jas felt like she was coming home.

She thought of the *Thylacine* as her ship. She was the only commander the relatively new vessel had ever had, and she had a sense of ownership of it. At five hundred and fifty meters long and half as wide, the *Thylacine* was only averagely sized compared to the rest of the Unity fleet, but the pulse cannons fore and aft were the latest and best technology. What was more, both the massive jump engine that underlay the working and residential quarters of the ship, and the smaller RaptorXs to either side were the fastest-responding that she'd ever known.

The engineer who had just completed his duty tour had maintained the engines in excellent working order, and Jas was confident that the person she suspected was his replacement would do the same. Like her namesake, the *Thylacine* was small compared to other predators of the Unity fleet, but she was deadly.

From behind Jas came the sounds of recruits whose stomachs were rebelling even more forcefully than hers at their abrupt arrival. She grimaced, and while the transport flew to the ship and through its bay doors, her mind dwelt on the person from her past and the events surrounding their acquaintance—friendship, even, though it hadn't started out that way.

Finally, the transport's engines powered down and the pilot comm'd to say it was safe to disembark. Jas unfastened her harness and stood up, turning to face the recruits. Some of the new crew members were pale and sweaty, and the cabin reeked from the small pools of vomit in the aisles. The cabin doors clicked and opened with a swoosh, allowing welcome filtered air into the vessel.

"Disembark from the back row forward," Jas said, "and line up in your sections outside."

The recruits stood and began pulling out their bags from the lockers, gingerly avoiding the puddles that dotted the floor. As Jas passed by, they stepped aside.

She went down the ramp and out into the launch bay, experiencing a sense of weird displacement caused by traveling by gateway and starjumping. She felt like she could have been aboard the *Thylacine* a few months ago or, as she had in fact, only a few hours ago. While she waited for the recruits to disembark, she checked over the bay doors. The repair crew had done a good job. The only evidence of the damage the second Shadow ship had inflicted was sprays of scorch marks across the inner bulkheads.

Krat. Jas remembered she'd meant to talk to Pacheco after the meeting about the odd occurrences in the *Thylacine's* most recent engagement. He hadn't seemed to pay much attention to the information while she was giving her report, and afterward she'd been focused on meeting the person from her past. She resolved to mail Pacheco later.

The new crew members were filing down the ramp and lining up as she'd told them. Jas scanned the crowd, her gaze finally alighting on the woman she was seeking. She was as stocky and ginger as ever, though fine lines on her pale face showed the passing of the years since they'd last known each other. Wealthier, or perhaps vainer individuals would have paid to have those wrinkles removed. It looked to Jas as though the woman's situation was similar to what it had been when they worked together.

As the woman met her gaze, Jas gave her a very brief smile.

"Who has the list of names?" she asked the waiting recruits. The defense units had organized themselves into a line too. Suddenly, Jas realized she'd spotted another familiar figure. "Wait a moment," she said as she went over to the AX unit. She read the unit's breastplate and looked up at the android's impassive face in surprise. "AX7. You worked with me aboard the *Galathea*."

"Yes, Commander Harrington."

"Do you remember?"

"Yes, Commander Harrington. All my memories are stored in my database."

Two members of the *Galathea's* crew had arrived on the Thylacine.

"I have the list here, ma'am," said the man who'd identified himself as highest-ranking among them earlier. He came over and handed her an interface.

Jas scanned the list. She would look at the details more closely later. At that moment, she was looking for only one name. She read it and the rank next to it. *Chief Engineer*. She nodded approvingly. It was as she expected. It would be good to have the woman aboard.

She told the new recruits to wait for their section officers, then asked her old acquaintance to go with her. They left the bay.

As soon as they were out of earshot of the others, Jas said, "Toirien, what a surprise to see you."

"You too, Jas...Commander," Toirien MacAdam replied.

Jas clicked her tongue. "No need to call me that. At least not while we're alone. I can't stand all that formality, but I have to go along with it."

"I recognized your name when they told me where I was going and who I'd be serving under," Toirien said, "but I wasn't sure it was really you until I saw you. Who'd have thought all those years ago that when we met again you'd be in command of a Unity destroyer?"

"A lot's happened since we were stuck on that Shadow trap planet," Jas said. "A lot." She hesitated. "Did you have to travel far to get to the Unity recruiting station? Are you tired?"

"No, not far," replied the engineer. "I'm not that tired."

"Do you want to join me for a drink and a chat after you settle in? I need to organize a few things, but then we could catch up on old times."

"Sure. I'd like that."

Jas led Toirien through the ship to the chief engineer's quarters and told her where to find her office when she was ready.

When Jas got back to her office, she drafted a long mail to Pacheco, reporting on the recent battle and highlighting the odd activity. She concluded,

Admiral, I'm concerned that the unfamiliar designs of the two Shadow ships, the unusual strength of the second ship's hull and

force field, the high caliber of its fighter pilots, and the ship's abrupt departure when it could have remained and possibly won the battle, are all significant.

Now that I've had time to process the details, it occurs to me that the Shadows may be moving beyond their strategy of using the skills, knowledge, and technology of their victims. They may be developing to be better than them. They could be building their own, better, ships, maybe even inventing new genetic enhancement techniques to improve their pilots' skills.

I suspect the Thylacine got off easy. I think the second ship jumped because they'd discovered what they wanted to know— that their technology is superior.

Jas's door chime sounded. She signed off the mail and sent it, then let Toirien in.

"What can I get you?" she asked, going to the drinks dispenser as the engineer took a seat.

"Water is fine," Toirien replied.

"Nothing stronger?"

"No, thanks. I haven't touched a drop of alcohol since that time you caught me off my face aboard the *Galathea*."

"Ha," Jas said. "I remember. Good for you." Toirien's alcohol and substance addiction had been a big problem, interfering with her work and judgment. Jas also recalled the engineer's wish that she could have her children returned to her. They'd been placed in care due to their mother's addictions.

She poured Toirien's water and ordered a mixed drink for herself. As she handed the beaker to the woman, she sat down on the other side of the desk. The engineer indicated Jas's drink and said, "Is it normal to have alcohol aboard a Unity vessel?"

"I allow it for special occasions," Jas replied. "A small

celebratory drink when we win a battle helps boost morale. It keeps my spirits up too."

Toirien's expression was doubtful, and she watched with concern as Jas took a sip of her drink. Jas noticed her look and attributed the engineer's unease to her own past history. It wasn't like that for Jas. Not everyone let their drinking get out of hand.

"So," she said, "who's looking after your kids while you're here?"

"They don't need anyone to look after them anymore. They're all grown up now. Fine young ladies. They've both signed up to fight. Joan is a comm technician and Grace has followed in her mam's footsteps. She's serving as an engineer aboard the *Camaradon*."

The *Camaradon* was Pacheco's command—the largest military space vessel ever built and the pride of the Unity fleet. It had been aboard the *Camaradon* that Jas had last seen Sayen Lee.

"It sounds like you set a great example, Toirien. You must be very proud of them."

Toirien's face twisted into an expression of regret. "I didn't do right by my children for a long time, but I hope I've made up for that at least a little over the last few years."

Jas took another sip of her drink, the alcohol easing some of the tension from her muscles. It was pleasant to talk with Toirien and slip into memories of past times. So much had happened since they last met, and her life was so different. She wondered if she was even the same person anymore.

"So, what's been happening with you?" Toirien asked. "How did you go from security officer on a private prospector to Unity commander? That must be quite a tale to tell."

Jas grimaced. "It is, and I'll tell you the whole story some time. But I'm curious to know about Earth. It's been a long while since I was there. What's been happening? How are things now?"

"Hmm...not too bad. You know that Earth was declared Shadow-free late last year? It was a long, hard struggle to root them all out, but we made it in the end. So many people died during their invasion. It was terrible. And toward the end as the entire population was being scanned, it was odd. People were clinging to their Shadow friends and family. Sheltering Shadows and hiding them from the authorities, in total self-denial. They couldn't face the fact that their loved ones were dead. The Shadows went along with the masquerade, of course, because the alternative was execution."

"How could they accept a Shadow in place of the person who'd been murdered?" Jas asked, shocked.

"I know how weird it sounds, but on the other hand, I know how easy it is to lie to yourself if you want to." Toirien glanced at the drink in Jas's hand.

"How's the recovery going?" Jas asked. "Are things getting back to normal?"

"Slowly, to be sure, but, yes, I'd say a kind of normality is returning to people's lives. Things are different now, though. Battling the Shadows has brought people together. Evened things out a little. You don't see the same separation between modded and naturals, for instance. A lot of the people who benefited from the divisions in societies, like the heads of corporations etcetera, they're nearly all dead. They were the ones the Shadows targeted. So it's like most of the very top layer of society was removed, and now people are trying to rebuild with a more equitable system. Basic modding for your baby is a right now, not a privilege. That'll continue to even things up. And there's more acceptance of people who choose a different way of life."

"That's good to hear." Jas recalled the underworlders and their struggle against a society that despised them. She wondered what Erielle thought of the changes.

Her interface chirruped. Pacheco had replied to her mail. "Excuse me a moment." She opened and read his message.

Thanks for your report. I've noted your concerns. Prepare to ship out to the coordinates given at our meeting. The Thylacine must be ready for action in eighty-four hours.

6

———

When Jas boarded the shuttle that would take her planetside, she was a little worse for wear after a long evening spent with Toirien. She took a seat in the cabin and comm'd the pilot that she was ready to go.

She'd talked with Toirien about old times and old acquaintances, like long-departed, myth-addicted Captain Loba, self-serving First Mate Haggardy, and bigoted Dr. Sparks. The engineer had been entertained to hear of what had happened to Sparks after leaving the *Galathea*. Jas wondered if anyone had told the doctor yet that Earth was finally free of Shadows, or if he was still hiding out the war at the chilly Ganymede Outpost.

She couldn't quite remember how her evening with Toirien had ended, but she'd woken with an aching head and sore stomach. She'd self-medicated to relieve the symptoms of her hangover, but she still felt light-headed and out of sorts. She hoped a visit to see how Trimborn was getting on with his Shadow sweep would distract her from her malaise.

Her first officer only had three days to train the locals in how to uncover the remaining Shadows hiding among them, and he had to do it effectively or the Shadows would regain control and a pocket of resistance would spring up.

The shuttle was sweeping rapidly down through the planet's atmosphere, buffeted by turbulence. Jas stretched her tender muscles and rubbed her eyes. She was tired, but it wasn't only due to her over-indulgence the night before. She'd been tired day in and day out for months—a deep-down tiredness that the longest sleep never seemed to fix.

"Touchdown in five, ma'am," came the pilot's voice through her comm.

Jas rested her head on the back of her seat and closed her eyes as the shuttle made its final approach. By the time it landed, she'd drifted into a light sleep. The sound of the cabin door opening roused her, and the sunlight that streamed in made her squint and blink. It was a brilliant light, and the air that entered the cabin was hot and dry.

Unfastening her harness, Jas stood and straightened her jacket. After smoothing down her hair at the back, she disembarked. Trimborn and a couple of his subordinates were waiting in a neat row a short distance away, but Jas was so blinded by the glaring light, she perceived them only as dark, indistinct figures.

She lifted a hand in front of her eyes to block out the sun, but the gesture didn't help much. The sun's brightness was reflected and seemingly multiplied by the surrounding landscape. She made her way over to her officers, her eyes narrowed to slits. Already, her uniform was feeling tight and uncomfortably warm.

"Good morning, ma'am," Trimborn said cheerfully as she approached.

"Morning...what are you wearing?" Jas asked.

Her first officer and the two other officers with him had cloths draped over their heads and down their backs. They were wearing their uniform hats, so the edges lifted the cloths into mini tents.

"Only thing that keeps the sun off, ma'am," Trimborn replied.

Jas noticed he also had on thick sunglasses.

The piercing light wasn't making her hangover any better. "Is there somewhere we can go?"

"Yes, Commander. This way." Trimborn led her toward a flat structure raised only a meter or so above the ground. She hadn't noticed it because it was yellow-tinged white, the same color as the rocky surrounding ground.

"You could have told me what to expect, Trimborn," Jas said as they walked together. "I would have come better prepared."

"I...er...I did, ma'am. I left a message as soon as I received notification you were coming down. But don't worry, once we're underground, it'll be fine."

Jas hadn't checked her messages after she'd gotten up that morning.

They arrived at a circular entrance with an overhanging roof, set halfway into the ground. There was no door, only a dark hole leading to the interior. Uneasiness settled on Jas, and for a moment she wasn't sure why. Then she realized.

"This is like a Shadow trap," she blurted. She grabbed at her side, but in her hungover state, she hadn't remembered to arm herself.

"Yes, it is, isn't it, ma'am," Trimborn said. "Gave us the willies at first too. But there's no cause for concern. It's perfectly safe."

But Jas stopped in her tracks, her legs trembling. The

last time she'd been near a Shadow trap, she'd been forced to watch people die while she stood by, helpless. And the time before that she'd had to kill the Shadow of someone she'd been close to.

She swallowed, fighting the urge to vomit.

"Commander," said Trimborn, taking off his sunglasses and peering at her, "are you feeling all right?"

She stared at her first officer. His ebony skin was glistening with sweat in the heat. Was he really who he seemed to be? Glancing at Trimborn's two subordinates, she began to back away. She tried to remember how far away and in which direction the shuttle stood.

Could she fight all three officers by herself? She was out of shape. She couldn't remember the last time she'd done any training.

"Commander," Trimborn said, "I think I understand your concerns, but we've followed all the protocols since landing. We are not Shadows."

She continued to step slowly backward out of the shade at the entrance until she was in the now-welcome, brilliant glare of the planet's sun. "I want proof. I want to scan you."

"But—" Trimborn protested.

"That's an order."

He shrugged, sighed, and turned to one of his subordinates. "Pop inside and bring out a scanner, would you?"

Jas and the remaining two officers waited in uncomfortable silence for the woman to return. Jas screwed up her eyes and hunched her shoulders in response to the pounding heat and sunlight.

Time passed, dragging its heels.

"The Shadow presence on this planet is minimal, ma'am," Trimborn said. "It's due to the Shadows' method of capturing their victims, I believe. The natives only rarely go above ground, you see, so it wasn't easy for the Shadows to entice them into their traps. And though the Shadow traps look similar to the local entrances to the underground cities, they look different enough to cause suspicion. Few victims would have entered willingly."

Jas didn't respond. She would talk to Trimborn when she knew for sure he *was* Trimborn.

The returning footsteps of the officer who had gone to collect a Shadow scanner broke the stillness and tension a little. The hand held scanner she'd brought was far smaller and easier to carry than the long, heavy, tube-shaped models the Council had manufactured in the beginning of the Shadow War. The officer handed the scanner to Jas and quickly returned to the shade.

She examined the device, running her fingers along its seams, checking for irregularities, such as if the instrument had been forced open. There *should* have been no way to open the scanners once they were sealed. They were designed to self-destruct if tampered with, so the chance the scanner had been fixed to give a false reading was remote, but it didn't hurt to check.

"Okay, one at a time, come over here so I can scan you," Jas said. "Trimborn, you first."

She ran the scanner down the back of her first officer. The mythranil inside it would react if Trimborn bore traces of that mysterious dimension where the Shadows existed. The display read *Clear*. Jas exhaled.

"Stand behind me," she told Trimborn. "You next."

It took just a few minutes to establish that neither of the remaining two officers were Shadows. She relaxed, but the headache she'd forgotten about returned. She handed back the scanner. "Okay, let's go in."

The entrance led into a tunnel not unlike the ones at the Transgalactic Council offices, except the walls were heavily decorated. The brilliant reflectiveness of the native rock, which seemed to be some kind of quartz, had been cut into complex, sophisticated patterns. As well as being entrancing to look at, the many angled surfaces seemed to have been cut to capture every last particle of light that entered from the surface, and transmit it deep underground.

As Jas's eyes adjusted to the gradually dimming light, she became more and more fascinated by the decoration, until she was compelled to stop and look at it more closely.

"Don't touch it, ma'am," Trimborn said. "It's devilishly sharp." He raised a hand to display thin scabs on his fingertips. "Not that the locals think so. One of them told me they like to scratch themselves against the walls. Beautiful, isn't it, though?"

"Scratch themselves?" Jas asked. "What are they like? I was thinking they must be a sort of arthropoid species, like the Council officers."

"Errmm...not exactly," Trimborn replied. He shared a meaningful glance with his fellow officers. "At least, not unless they have another stage to their life cycle. But you'll meet them in a moment, Commander. We're nearly there."

They continued for another few minutes, until they reached a slope in the ground that led to a hole roughly half as wide as the tunnel.

"This leads to some kind of governmental area attached to a mine," Trimborn said. "Careful when you get to the bottom." He sat down at the edge of the slope and pushed off. He slid down and disappeared through the hole. The other officers did the same, and Jas followed last of all.

Though she'd encountered a wide variety of aliens over her career as a security officer and then in deep space military service, she couldn't suppress the revulsion she felt when she saw what awaited them at the bottom of the tunnel.

7

Jas emerged into a domed chamber. At first glance, the place seemed to be full of human-sized maggots. The sentient species of the mythrin-bearing planet were long and plump, and they seemed to be segmented, according to what was visible of their bodies. They wore patterned and plain one-piece skin-like coverings in a variety of styles and colors.

At one end of the creatures was a star-shaped opening that they flexibly moved, and surrounding the opening was a circle of black dots. The dots seemed to be eyes, because they turned toward Jas, Trimborn, and the others. Folds of skin swept over the dots, covering and uncovering them, apparently randomly.

The creatures moved by edging forward on their lower halves, born along on waves of movement that originated at their heads and progressed down their bodies. It was this style of locomotion, plus the fat, segmented bodies, that turned Jas's stomach. The natives' resemblance to maggots was so strong, she found it hard to push the thought out of her mind during her entire visit.

Though she'd forgotten her weapon, she had, at least, remembered her comm. She switched on its translation function and fought the urge to step back as the aliens edged closer, uttering greetings and thanks for releasing them from the Shadows' control of their planet.

Around the walls of the chamber, hammocks were slung for some reason, and they were filled with yet more of the creatures. At Jas's and the other officers' appearance, they had begun to wriggle out and drop to the floor with soft squelching sounds. These individuals also edged over eagerly, so closely that they were rubbing up against each other.

Trimborn introduced Jas to the creatures, then said, "Ma'am, this is Head of Nest of this nation." He added under his breath, "The translators can't seem to handle their names, but it doesn't appear to matter."

"The Unity Alliance accepts your thanks," Jas said, "but it's unneeded. As members of the Transgalactic Council, you are entitled to military aid in the case of invasion. We only regret that we couldn't free your planet sooner. May I ask how the implementation of the Shadow Sweep protocols is progressing?"

"Well, well, very well," the Head of Nest replied. "Your scanners are working very well. We've found many Shadows. They are very delicious. Thank you. Thank you."

Jas's already sensitive stomach turned over. She caught a glimpse of Trimborn's smirk from the corner of her eye.

"You're...welcome. I'm glad to hear that things are progressing quickly. I'm here to inform you that I must withdraw my team from your world soon. We can supply you with more scanners if you need them, but after the training period is over, you must cooperate with the other nations of your planet to detect any remaining Shadows. Are you confident that your citizens will be able to implement the protocols effectively?"

"Yes, yes. Your trainers teach very well. We understand what to do, and we will do it. Thank you. Thank you."

Jas nodded. She would have to see Trimborn's assessment report before taking the alien's word for it.

"One more thing," she went on. "The Shadow ship that we destroyed, was it from this planet?"

"Yes, yes. It was from here."

"So it was one of your starships?"

"No, no. Not one of ours. The Shadows built it here. Imported materials. We don't build starships from metal. We make them from..." Jas's comm emitted a tone that meant it was unable to translate the word.

"I see," she said. "Thank you for the information."

She concentrated on the Head of Nest—the one non-moving alien in front of her. The creatures' squirming around was increasing her nausea.

"Um," she said, trying to think up a reason to cut the visit short. "I appreciate you taking the time to meet with me, but I have urgent business to take care of, so—"

"Yes, yes. You're very busy. We understand. But we would like to show you a little of our home and what we do here, if you can spare the time. Thank you. Thank you."

Jas hesitated. Right now, she wanted nothing more than to return to the baking overground, the shuttle, and the *Thylacine*.

"I think I know what it means," Trimborn said. "It's very interesting, ma'am. Won't take long, I think."

Jas studied her first officer. A trace of the man's earlier smirk remained. Was he setting her up for something? But she was feeling too under the weather to think up a suitably polite refusal to tell the Head of Nest. Political diplomacy was just about her worst skill as a Unity commander.

She swallowed.

"I would love to see more of your home," she said.

Along with its group, the creature turned and squirmed away. Jas assumed she was supposed to follow, and set off after them, checking that Trimborn and the others were coming along too.

"What's this about?" she asked Trimborn quietly as he drew level with her.

"If it's the same thing they showed us before," he replied, "they're taking us to see their mythrin mine. I thought it was fascinating. Well worth an hour or so, if you can spare it, ma'am."

She took a deep breath and exhaled, which made her feel a little better. "Okay. Let's do it."

The Head of Nest had brought them to a door like an old-style camera lens. It opened automatically as they neared it, and the eyes of the aliens glowed to light up the dark tunnel beyond. This tunnel was smooth white rock, lacking the decoration of the entrance tunnel. The surface lightly reflected the beams from the creatures' eyes, creating a shimmering effect.

In other circumstances, Jas thought to herself, she would have enjoyed exploring this planet—its unsightly sentient species aside.

She and her officers followed the undulating Head of Nest as the tunnel sloped sharply down, until Jas was leaning backward in an effort not to slip. The creatures didn't seem to have a problem with the angle. In fact, some of them began wriggling along the walls in defiance of gravity.

When the floor finally evened out, they stopped. They'd

arrived at the end of the tunnel, though in the walls opposite were two smaller holes, linked by a strip of highly polished, flat ground.

The Head of Nest said, "Waiting, waiting. Thank you. Thank you."

A sound of rushing wind was coming from one of the holes in the wall, and within a few moments the source of the sound appeared. It was a torpedo-shaped cart made of a hard, stony material, and it hovered a centimeter or two above the ground.

Following the Head of Nest's lead, Jas got in the cart along with her officers. The seating was made to fit the locals' body shape, so they had to recline on it rather than sit. As soon as everyone was in, the cart whooshed off.

Jas looked around, trying to understand how the vehicle was moving.

"I couldn't figure it out either, ma'am," Trimborn said.

They were borne along at an increasingly fast speed until the ceiling and sides of the tunnel whizzed past them. Jas was careful to keep her head well down and her arms and legs tucked in. The long, low body shape of the natives made their danger of being hurt much lower. Whenever the vehicle tilted upward or downward at a sharp angle, the creatures' bodies or clothing also prevented them from slipping out, while Jas had to grip on to the edge of her seat. She was reminded of rare visits to amusement parks when she was in the institute for cared-for children on Earth. The experience did, at least, take her mind off her nausea.

The ride slowed as quickly as it had begun when they arrived at a landing place. Jas climbed out of the cart, her legs wobbly. They were in a similar place to the one they'd just left, but the rock surface was more roughly hewn.

"This is one of our oldest seams," the Head of Nest told her, "yet it remains productive. Yes. Yes."

The creature led them down yet another tunnel. This one bore markings along the ceiling, which seemed to be notices or signs. Jas wondered how much farther they had to go. Her neck ached from stooping in the low tunnel. Trimborn had said the trip would take an hour or so, and they'd already been traveling for around twenty-five minutes.

As she was about to ask if their destination was much farther, the Head of Nest stopped.

"Here it is. Here it is," the alien announced.

Jas and her officers were at the back of the group. She looked around, wondering what she was supposed to be seeing. Trimborn nudged her. The aliens in front of them were shuffling sideways, creating a gap for them to pass through. She went forward.

The Head of Nest said, "Welcome. Welcome. See."

She followed the direction of its glowing eyes to a spot on the wall. A tube was fixed there below a tiny crack. The tube was the same color and material as the wall, which was why she'd failed to see it at first.

"That's it, ma'am," Trimborn said, arriving at her side.

"That's it?" Jas asked.

"Yes. Look inside the tube."

She leaned forward until her forehead was nearly resting on the wall. Deep down in the tube, a liquid glinted in the glow from the assembled aliens' eyes. The liquid was a delicate, pale pink. She noticed that at the edge of the crack above the tube, a drop of the liquid had swelled. As she watched, the drop fell. Simultaneously, the collected aliens' bodies trembled.

"This is it. This is it," the Head of Nest said. "Mythrin is our world's main source of income. We do not use it. Our bodies do not metabolize it. We only collect it and sell it. Very valuable. Yes. Yes."

The color of the mythrin was much paler than the deep scarlet of mythranil, but that made sense. Mythranil was the refined drug and mythrin was only the raw ingredient. Yet seeing the drug in its natural state made Jas shiver. The narcotic sent the user temporarily to the home of the Shadows, the Void, and it was vital for its use in Shadow scanners.

Also, they'd come a distance of kilometers deep underground to witness the collection of a single drop. No wonder the drug cost so much.

As they traveled back through the mythrin mine, Trimborn told Jas what he'd learned about mythrin from the natives of the planet: that only a particular combination of rare factors, including unusual geological formations and eons-long processes, would result in small amounts of the chemical oozing out of the rock.

"They didn't even know they had mythrin on the planet," he went on. "A couple of geologists who were scouting around found it. They tried to keep the discovery a secret, but the locals soon figured out what they were mining. Booted the geologists off the planet, or possibly ate them. They were vague about that part. Anyway, the local governments weren't slow to exploit the new source of income. Now, according to one Head of Nest anyway, no one living on the planet need ever work again. Except for the miners, of course, and they receive double income."

Trimborn chattered on after Jas had thanked the aliens and said goodbye. He went with her to the shuttle. She barely registered what he was saying, and as she returned to the *Thylacine*, her mind was deeply occupied.

The sight of the mythrin hadn't only caused her to feel

wonder. Though it had been five years since the one time she'd experienced the effects of mythranil, her memory of the experience remained strong. Her close proximity to its raw ingredient had created in her a deep desire to use it again.

The feeling of need for the illegal drug, together with her alcoholic binge the previous evening, her constant tiredness, and her inability to consider her future, as if she just didn't care anymore what happened, brought her to another personal truth: she was beginning to fall apart.

8

When Jas arrived at her office aboard the *Thylacine,* a mail from Pacheco was awaiting her. He was requesting a face-to-face meeting, but this time he would come to her. The time he proposed was soon.

Jas sent her acceptance. The timing wasn't great—she would have preferred longer to prepare her thoughts—but she was glad the admiral had taken her concerns about the Shadow ship seriously. She left a note on the general system to say where she could be found, and waited.

The green motes of the gateway appeared in the air in the corner of her office. When the spiral was swirling strongly, the black-uniformed leg of the admiral appeared, soon followed by the rest of his body. He gave her a nod and took off his hat. Behind him, the gateway disappeared like water running down a plug hole.

"Jas," he said, coming forward.

"Admiral Pacheco," Jas replied. "Thank you for coming. I guess you must be very busy with the battle coming up. Please take a seat." She sat behind her desk. "I take it that this is about my mail? Did any of the other commanders notice anything similar? What do you think about it? Are you going to modify the battle plans?"

Pacheco was putting his hat down and hitching up his trousers before sitting as Jas spoke. He gave her a quizzical look and an embarrassed half smile. He rested his hands on his knees.

"I read your report, Jas, and I agree what you saw is odd, but the battle plan is complex, involving thousands of Unity Alliance ships and hundreds of thousands of personnel. We're too far along to change anything now, even if your observations are correct. What do they mean anyway? That the Shadows have their own ships and very well trained pilots? I'm not sure how that's going to change anything that we should or could do."

"Of course it should affect what we do. If they're building their own ships, we could try to find out their specs. We could gather more intelligence in Shadow-controlled planets. If this is our best chance to defeat them, like you said, shouldn't we make the best preparations we can?"

"Does something make you think we aren't already gathering intelligence on Shadow-controlled planets?" Pacheco asked. "I can tell you we've received no information about them building their own ships. Why would they need to when they can just take their victims'? It takes years to build new ships. Don't forget they only have the knowledge and skills of the people they murder. If they were designing new ships, we would have seen more evidence of it than a couple of vessels in a minor battle. Battleships aren't exactly easy to hide."

"But what if they have?" Jas asked. "The technology I observed on one of the ships was much better than ours. If we go ahead without knowing more, the next battle could be suicide for us."

"If they do have a few starships that are better than ours, the sooner we annihilate them, the better." Pacheco tutted and shook his head. "Jas, you're not getting it. It's too late to do anything now. The countdown's begun and the wheels are turning. A little under three days from now, every available ship in the Unity Alliance fleet will jump into strategically decided coordinates, and the battle will commence. The last battle, I hope."

Her tension deflated with disappointment. She was sure there was something to be learned from what she'd seen, something important and worth acting upon, but it was clear she wouldn't persuade the admiral of it.

"Then," she said with a frown, "why are you here?"

Pacheco picked up his hat and began turning it in his hands. He looked down at it as he seemed to think about how to answer her.

"Let's forget about me being an admiral and you being a commander for a moment, okay?" he said at last. "We go back a long way, Jas, don't we? Do you remember when we first met?"

Her heart sank. So *this* was why he'd come. Couldn't the man take a hint?

"Yes," she replied, "of course I do. You were serving on the *Infineon*, and I'd been sent there in command of a team of defense units. Some of the ship's pilots died rescuing us when our transport was attacked."

Pacheco nodded. "I was quite upset about that. We were short of pilots as it was, and to lose some over a handful of defense units and a single greenhorn, well, it didn't seem worth it. Not that it was your fault."

Jas replied. "I don't think it was my fault either, but I felt bad about those pilots too. And all those who have died since."

"I know you do. I know," Pacheco said softly. His gaze returned to his hat.

She was squirming with embarrassment on the man's behalf, though she didn't know what she could do to avert him from the course he'd set upon.

"When the Shadows in the *Infineon's* crew revealed themselves, and the fight erupted on the bridge," he continued, "and Commander Torbin was killed, you and I were pinned down in one spot together...do you remember?"

"Yes, you got that horrible burn on your side from metal heated by laser fire."

"That wasn't so bad." He paused. "I changed my mind about you during that fight. I saw how hard and how bravely you fought. I knew the effort to save you had been worth it."

She sighed. She wasn't so sure about that.

"And since then," Pacheco said, "we've served together most of the time. How many of us are left who have been in the war since the start, do you think? Not many, I guess."

He gave a huff of frustration and put his hat down on the seat next to him.

Here it comes. Jas looked with sympathy into the man's dark, troubled eyes.

"What I'm trying to say is," Pacheco said, "over the years, I've grown to care about you. Probably more than you think. And I wanted to come here and tell you so because in a few days' time we'll both be involved in something that's going to decide the fate of the galaxy. Who knows if either of us will survive?

"It seemed important that I tell you how I feel," he continued as Jas was wishing she could disappear into the floor. "I guess I'm here to find out if there's anything I can hope for when it's all over. I'm not sure exactly what I mean to you, Jas, but I don't think you feel the same way about me as I do about you. That's what's always stopped me from saying something. But I believe it's wrong to sit on these things forever. So here I am."

He looked up, all the dignity and demeanor of his office and rank stripped away.

Her heart ached for him, but not in the way he clearly hoped. She opened her mouth to speak, but he interrupted her, her expression apparently telling him everything he needed to know.

"It's someone from your past, isn't it," he said heavily. "Someone from before we met. I noticed you've never gotten together with anyone in all this time. I saw how eagerly you scanned your new recruits after I told you an old acquaintance was among them, and how your face fell when you didn't see whoever it was you were hoping to find."

"My private life is my own concern," Jas said quietly.

The admiral's disappointed features became hard and set. He stood and picked up his hat. "So you *are* clinging to the past, like I thought. In that case, you're a fool. You're wasting away your life on a memory when you could be happy. If you would just give someone else a chance, you could be loved. Did you ever consider that?"

Her hands clenching into fists at his attack, Jas also moved to stand but in her haste she banged her knees on her desk. She gave a gasp of pain and sat down again, her hands on her lower thighs. "Krat, Pacheco. Things aren't that simple. I don't get to choose how I feel."

The admiral stepped toward her and stood over her, his black-suited figure shading out the overhead light. "You're living in the past, Jas. Living on dreams." He squatted down, looked up into her eyes, and continued in a more conciliatory tone, "When we win this battle, things will go back to normal. People will return home and pick up the pieces. Build new lives. Start anew. We always worked well together, Jas. You can't deny it. We think alike. We have a good rapport. When all this is over, you and I would make a good team. And I know you don't hate me. If you would just stop shutting me out, we could have something good going for us, don't you think?"

She looked down and didn't answer. She couldn't answer. In some ways, he was right, but so was she when she'd said she didn't have a choice about how she felt.

He gave a sigh of exasperation and stood up. "So that's it, is it? We go into battle with no hope for a future? You're content with that? What's the point then? Who is it you're fighting for?"

Still, she had no words of reply, but the response that popped into her mind was, *not me.*

9

———

The pilots had assembled in the launch bay as Jas had requested prior to what she hoped would be the final battle. The old hands would know what was coming, but she made them attend anyway. Her words were just as important however often they heard them.

She always spoke to the pilots on the eve of every battle. Though it tortured her to look into the eyes of the men and women standing before her, knowing that many of them would be dead within a few short hours, she felt they were owed this personal address. It was the very least someone like her, who would be within relative safety behind the force field and heavy hull plating of a starship, could do.

They deserved acknowledgment of the risk they were taking, and for many, of the sacrifice they would make, so that others could live in peace and safety.

For Jas, it meant more than that. She forced herself to look into the eyes of the people she was effectively sending out to die because she didn't want to become hardened to their fate. She wanted to be sure those women and men were real to her, so she would never deploy them unless it was absolutely necessary.

The pilots were dressed in their flight suits and standing to attention. The fresh recruits' uniforms were new and colored a deep, rich gray. Older pilots were identifiable by their lighter gray suits, faded a little with time.

"At ease, pilots," Jas said. "This won't take long." She put her hands in her pockets. "As you know, tomorrow we begin a new battle. I can't emphasize to you enough how important it is that you have one hundred percent confidence in your ships. Before you go to bed tonight, I want each and every one of you to be absolutely certain that your ship and all your equipment is in perfect working order."

Her comm button bleeped, but she ignored it.

"If you're uncertain about anything, or if you want to run another diagnostic, ask a technician. If any of them complain they're too busy or not on duty, report them to me. Have you got that?" She stopped her pacing and glared at the pilots, who gave a few hesitant replies of *Yes, Commander.*

Her comm button bleeped again.

"*Krat it*," she muttered under her breath. Lifting the button to her lips, she barked, "What?"

It was Trimborn. "Commander, Navigator Curlio's violently ill. I've sent her to the sick bay."

"What?" Jas repeated. "What's wrong with her?"

"I don't know, ma'am. She keeled over at her station. She's running a fever and delirious. The doctor's assessing her at the moment."

Jas hoped the woman's illness wasn't serious and that, whatever it was, it wasn't contagious. The ship's crew coming down with a virus just before going into battle was the last thing she needed. As it was, the best-case scenario was her navigator would be out of commission for the next few, crucial, hours.

She ran through her mental list of the ship's company, trying to think of a replacement. She didn't know of anyone aboard with recent experience of navigating a destroyer, and when she asked Trimborn, neither did he. They could use someone who had out-of-practice navigation skills, but there might still be time to find a better solution.

"Direct comm Admiral Pacheco, Trimborn," Jas said, "and explain the situation. Maybe someone's available who can replace Curlio at short notice."

"Yes, ma'am."

She closed her eyes for a moment to refocus on her speech to the pilots.

"You've got the hardest, most dangerous job of all to do tomorrow," she continued. "I'm sure you realize that, but you're still here, and that says a lot. You chose to join this war, and you chose the riskiest way to serve. Every one of you standing in this bay is already a hero. I want you to understand that I and everyone else aboard this ship knows it and we appreciate what you're doing.

"I also want to thank you, now, for your service, and to tell you that I will do everything in my power to bring every single one of you home again to your families and loved ones. Good luck, everyone. Dismissed."

At her command, the pilots broke formation. Some began to walk away, but a few came over to her. The first held out his hand. He was a short, slightly tubby man with silvered stubble. He was wearing the fresh uniform of a recruit, yet he looked too old to enlist. Jas guessed the recruiting officers made exceptions for those with flying experience.

She shook the man's hand. The woman who was with

him also held out her hand, and the next pilot, and the next. The ones who were leaving noticed what was happening, and they came back to also shake her hand.

She was so moved, she couldn't speak. Her lips drawn to a thin line, she shook each pilot's hand. When they were all done, she waited where she was and watched the courageous women and men leave the launch bay. She hoped they would spend the next few hours as well as they could before they began the fight of their lives.

10

———

Sayen Lee was deep in concentration when her comm sounded. She was sitting at her cabin's interface screen manually calculating starjumps. It was an old habit from the days when she worked aboard prospecting starships. The mental exercise calmed her and distracted her from excessive worrying about her brother, Phelan, who was heavily involved in rooting out the remaining Shadows on Earth.

She'd been figuratively kicking her heels aboard the *Camaradon* for the last two weeks, and she'd gotten increasingly bored. Admiral Pacheco had assigned her the role of second navigator after the frigate she'd served aboard last had been incapacitated in a skirmish. But the *Camaradon's* first navigator was entirely competent at his job as well as irritated by her hanging around. Effectively, she had krat all to do.

"Navigator Lee," came the admiral's voice over her comm. "You're being reassigned. Get ready to ship out. You'll be leaving by gateway in thirty minutes."

"Yes, sir," Sayen replied. "Permission to ask where I'm going, Admiral?"

"The *Thylacine*. Their navigator's taken ill and they don't have a suitable replacement."

"Thank you, sir," exclaimed Sayen, but the admiral had already broken the connection.

The *Thylacine* was Jas's command. Sayen was sure that was what she'd heard. Throughout the Shadow War personal comms had been strictly forbidden for security reasons. The risk of vital information leaking out was too high. As a result, Sayen hadn't sent or received a word from her friend for five years. It had only been when Jas's rapid rise to the rank of commander became a topic of gossip that Sayen had known she was still alive.

And now, after all this time, she would see her again.

It took Sayen only ten minutes to prepare to leave. It didn't take long to pack when all your belongings were neatly arranged in drawers and your cabin was already spotless and tidy. She shouldered her regulation duffle bag and trotted through the ship to the gateway door.

She knew the destination well. It had been at the same gateway door that Sayen had arrived aboard the *Camaradon* when she'd signed up to fight all those years ago. She recalled the massive bay holding the huge military transports and the crowds of volunteers of all species who were flooding in to join what everyone had seemed to think would be a short fight.

She and Jas had been assigned to different vessels, and her last glimpse of her tall, Martian friend had been as she left to command a team of defense units. Jas had been upset that her sweetheart, Carl, had volunteered before them. Sayen also hadn't seen Carl for five years. She hoped that he and Jas had met again in the intervening time.

She navigated the *Camaradon's* passageways with ease. To give herself something to do during her enforced break from work, she'd explored the battleship from top to bottom. It was an impressive vessel, nearly a kilometer long. Its size meant that it required two sets of starjump engines, and they were positioned to each side of the central working and living areas. The largest pulse cannons were fixed onto the engines to better utilize their energy generation capabilities if the ship's stored power ran low. During a space battle, the *Camaradon* could continue firing long after lesser vessels had exhausted their power.

Sayen arrived at the gateway entrance. The alien guard in charge scanned her embedded chip and said, "You're early, but you can go now if you want."

Sayen nodded, excited at the thought of being reunited with her old friend. They'd been through so much together.

The guard started up the gateway. It was only the second time Sayen had traveled via the Transgalactic Council's classified technology, usually reserved only for high-ranking individuals on urgent business. At the guard's signal, she stepped into the mist and out into the reception area of the *Thylacine.*

She'd half-expected Jas to meet her, but there was only a young first officer who introduced himself as Trimborn. She guessed Jas didn't know who Pacheco had sent as a replacement navigator.

"Boy am I glad to see you," Trimborn said. "We were waiting all night for the admiral to send us a replacement navigator. I guess he's busy preparing for the battle. I'll show you to your cabin. After you drop off your stuff, I'll take you directly to the bridge. We don't have long before we go into battle, and I'm sure you'll want to familiarize yourself with the *Thylacine's* controls."

"I would, thanks," Sayen replied.

She matched the officer's quick pace as they did as he'd said. As they went along, she took in the attitude of the crew and the general state of the ship. Everyone seemed to know what they were doing, and there was no slouching about or time wasting. All seemed in good order. The *Thylacine* was shipshape and ready for battle. But then Sayen expected no less with Jas in command.

She thought she'd have a little fun with the first officer.

"Hey, Trimborn," she said, "would I be out of line to ask what Commander Harrington's like? I heard she has quite a reputation."

The first officer twisted his lips in a slight grimace as he considered his answer. "Let me put it like this: the commander's a bit of a dragon, truth be told, but the crew have a helluva lot of respect for her. Some commanders I've served under seemed to think of losing crew as unfortunate but necessary collateral damage, but not Harrington. You know that when it comes down to it, she's got your back, if you know what I mean."

"Yeah, I know what you mean," Sayen replied. "I think so too."

"Wait a minute," Trimborn said, "I thought you hadn't served under her."

"I haven't, but I know her from way back before the War started."

Trimborn sucked air between his teeth and looked at her from the corners of his eyes. "I guess I'm lucky I didn't say anything worse. Is what I said going to get back to her?"

"Don't worry. Commander Harrington wouldn't give a damn whether anyone thought she was a dragon. She might even take it as a compliment."

She put her duffle bag on the bunk in her new cabin and

followed the first officer to the bridge. The bridge doors parted, and Sayen stepped through into the familiar setting. Over the years, she'd served aboard several Unity ships. The sight that interested her was the figure sitting in the commander's seat with her back toward her.

Sayen would have recognized Jas's tall figure and short, reddish-brown brown hair anywhere.

"Commander," Trimborn said, "our replacement navigator has arrived."

"Good," Jas replied without looking around. "Take your seat, Navigator. We're running through pre-engagement checks."

"Yes, Commander," Sayen replied with a smile. She went to the empty navigator's station and sat down. With a sweep of her hand, she activated her interface and bent over it, wondering how long it would take for the penny to drop.

When she glanced in Jas's direction, she saw her friend staring at her, the light of realization dawning on her face. Her mouth opened then shut abruptly as she appeared to remember where she was.

For the next hour, Sayen and the rest of the officers on the bridge ran through the battle prep, testing and retesting their controls. Jas led them through it, her demeanor calm. Occasionally, her and Sayen's gazes would meet briefly, but they stayed in their professional roles while the process was completed.

"Thanks, everyone," Jas said finally. "Please remain at your stations while we await the order to jump. Shouldn't be long now. Navigator Lee, I'd like to speak with you for a moment."

Sayen got up to follow Jas out of the bridge, but her pleasure at meeting her friend again was tinged with concern.

While the officers had been carrying out the checks,

she'd had time to see how much Jas had changed. When Sayen had known her, she'd exuded vitality and strength. But her impression of her old friend this time around had shocked her. Jas was thin, and she'd lost her previously firm, well-muscled physique. What was more, stress and exhaustion were written into her features. She looked like she hadn't slept properly in days.

Worse than all this was something else, something that underlay all of the other signs of a long-serving, overworked Unity commander. What jumped out at Sayen about Jas was that she seemed to be living with a deep sadness.

11

———

As soon as they reached a passageway that was empty, Jas grabbed Sayen into a hug. She was half-tempted to lift the petite woman off of her feet and swing her around, but she guessed that Sayen might find that undignified.

As she let go of her, she exclaimed, "When Pacheco said he was sending me another navigator, I didn't guess for a second it would be you. Where have you been all this time? What have you been doing? Ough." She let out a gasp of frustration. "Why does it have to be now, right before a battle, that we get to see each other again? I wish we had more time to talk."

"Me too," Sayen replied. "But forget what I've been doing, what have *you* been doing? You're a commander now. That's amazing."

Jas made a self-deprecating *meh*. "I had inside help, I think. Look at you, though. You haven't changed a bit. You look exactly the same as you did five years ago."

"That's no surprise," Sayen replied. "The doctors who

created my enhanced skin told me it doesn't age, so I'm gonna look like this until I die."

A crew member appeared around a bend in the corridor, and both women became silent. Jas had hunched over to talk quietly to her short friend, but at the sight of the man she drew herself up. As soon as he had passed them and disappeared around the next bend, she returned to her former position.

"Guess what," she said, "Toirien MacAdam's aboard too. Do you remember her? She was the only engineer aboard the *Galathea* who survived the Shadow attack and the crash."

Sayen said, "Yeah, I remember hearing about her. How's she doing?"

Jas briefly filled her in on Toirien's life story since she'd returned to Earth. "It seems weird that the three of us should come together again just before this final battle. There's even an old defense unit from the *Galathea* aboard." She looked pensive.

"The final battle?" Sayen asked, her eyes wide.

"Krat," Jas said. "I was forgetting you didn't know. I'm not supposed to tell the crew, but yeah, this next engagement is the final push. We've got them on the run, Sayen. We're almost there. The remaining Shadow force is confined to one small sector of the galaxy. We've wiped them out everywhere else, and if we can defeat their last ships now, the war's over for them. We'll have to do some mopping up, but that'll basically be it. Every Unity Alliance ship in service is being deployed. The *Camaradon's* leading the fight."

Jas's comm bleeped. It was Pacheco. "Commander Harrington, prepare to starjump at thirteen hundred and fifty."

"Affirmative, Admiral," Jas replied. They had a little

under half an hour. As always before an engagement with the enemy, Jas's heart began to race, but it had already been beating fast while she'd been talking to Sayen, and not only because she was excited to see her old friend again.

"How's Phelan?" she asked, skirting around the question she was burning but also fearing to ask.

"He's okay," Sayen replied. "Busy finding the remaining few Shadows on Earth. That was the last I heard from a recruit who'd heard of him. It's hard to keep track of what's happening when no comms are allowed. I hate having no contact with him."

"And Erielle?"

Sayen heaved a deep, sad sigh. "Erielle died not long after she returned to Earth with Makey."

"Oh krat, Sayen. I'm so sorry."

"Thanks. I found out a couple of years ago when I was allowed a short trip home. She died not long after she got back. It was Shadows among her underworlders. An inside job, not an open fight." Sayen's shoulders were sagging, but she straightened up as she added, "But Makey's doing well. He survived the fight for the control of Earth, and now he heads some kind of underworlders' council, negotiating for the rights of naturals."

"That's good to hear," Jas said. "Good for him. He was always a special kid."

"Yeah, he was."

After a slight pause, Jas finally found the courage to ask about their other mutual friend, but as she spoke, so did Sayen.

"Have you seen—" Jas asked at the same time that Sayen also asked,

"Do you know what—"

They both stopped speaking. Jas realized what Sayen's question meant.

"You mean you don't know what's happened to Carl?" she asked.

Sayen shook her head. "I haven't seen him since Ganymede Outpost. Have you?"

"No," Jas replied. "Not once."

"Jas, I'm really sorry."

She swallowed. "I guess that's it, then. He couldn't have survived all this time."

Sayen touched her arm. "You don't know that. Have you searched the personnel records?"

"I don't have security access, and the records are all over the place anyway. He's gone, Sayen. He has to be dead."

"Don't give up hope. Not while there's still a chance."

"He's a pilot, Sayen. Do you know of a pilot who's been around since the beginning of the war? What are the chances that he's still alive?"

Sayen looked down and gave a slight shake of her head. "I don't know what to say. I can't believe it. I thought you'd tell me that you'd seen him."

"And I guess you were my last hope." Jas continued to herself, "Pacheco was right."

"What do you mean?" Sayen asked.

"Just something the admiral said." She heaved a large sigh. "We don't have long before we jump. Let's go back to the bridge."

12

———

Admiral Pacheco adjusted the collar of his uniform and placed his arms gently on his arm rests. As he surveyed the officers at their consoles on the bridge of the *Camaradon*, his body thrummed with tension. He was careful not to let it show, however. During his long career serving with the Unity, he'd learned that a crew took their cue from whoever was in charge—commander, captain, or admiral. If he wanted his women and men to feel confident, confidence was what he had to exude.

Not that he wasn't confident. Though it had taken five years to get to this point, the Unity Alliance had been successful in slowly gaining ground and destroying their enemy, forcing them into this corner of the galaxy. In the forthcoming battle, the UA had every chance of delivering the final, crushing blow.

He wasn't tense because he thought they were in danger of losing. It was because he was responsible for the maneuvers of more than sixty starships as they battled the Shadows.

It was the largest number of ships that had been under

his command all at once, and it would take every ounce of concentration and skill to do his job. The battleground was vast. He was only one of many peers performing the same role across the sector. In all, the Unity Alliance had amassed more than one thousand starships to fight this final battle.

Save for a few frigates busy stamping out flares of Shadow resurgence on distant worlds, the entire Unity fleet was present. But the Unity ships numbered only in the hundreds. The rest of the force was made up of Alliance vessels and crews from across all of galactic civilization. The many and varied alien species from high- and low-g planets, water worlds, ice giants, desert orbs, and the other multitude of homes to sentient life scattered across the galaxy, had come together to defeat their common enemy.

It was a coordinated effort that would be remembered for thousands of years to come, providing they won the day. And they would. Pacheco was sure of it.

After the battle, he planned to leave the service. Too long a career space officer, he was tired of fighting. If only Jas Harrington's affections didn't lie with some probably long-dead lover from her past, he pondered. He wasn't a man to form frivolous connections. His feelings toward the Martian had grown over the years that they'd worked together aboard his first command ship.

Their first encounter had been rocky but, as time went on, he'd learned to appreciate her steady, effective approach to her work as well as her personal integrity. Before long, he'd realized he was giving her responsibilities much above her rank because he knew with certainty he could always rely on her.

When career progressions meant they'd parted ways, he'd soon missed her presence on a professional level and, in the quiet of his bunk at night, he'd realized he also missed *her*. He wished she could reciprocate his feelings. He wanted to relieve that constant melancholic look she always wore. He wanted to make her happy.

Pacheco shifted in his seat and checked the time. Fifteen minutes before his fleet was scheduled to jump to their designated positions and attack the Shadow ships known to be hiding out at certain coordinates. The *Camaradon* was going to engage with the leading ship. Everything was in place. The battle plan was laid out. All they had to do was follow it. What would happen afterward, Pacheco wasn't sure. Perhaps he shouldn't give up hope of winning Jas over just yet.

The doors opened, and Fleet Admiral Tarsa entered the bridge. A Haidiren, she was encased in her water-holding suit, her grass-green head poking from the top into a transparent, globe helmet. Pacheco and his officers stood to attention and saluted.

The alien's v-shaped lips quivered, which her translator related as, "Admiral Pacheco, I came in person to wish you and your officers good fortune in the forthcoming engagement."

"Thank you, Fleet Admiral," Pacheco replied.

"Your planning has been meticulous. We have every chance of success. I am now withdrawing to my private rooms to oversee the battle as a whole. If I have instructions for you, or if you wish to consult me, we will use the ship's comm."

"Very good, Fleet Admiral," said Pacheco.

"Good luck, everyone," Tarsa said to the bridge generally. "You couldn't wish for a better leader than Admiral Pacheco here. I leave you in his capable hands."

As the Fleet Admiral left, his officers returned their attention to their consoles and Pacheco took his seat again.

They had ten minutes. He checked with his first officer that he was ready to bring up a holo of the battleground the second that they jumped.

"Yes, Admiral," came the reply, with a slight hurt tone underlying it.

Pacheco tutted softly over his officer's response. Some people were over-sensitive. Of course, the man knew his job, and Pacheco hadn't meant to imply that he didn't. He tapped his armrests, his fingernails hitting the interface screens. Time seemed to slow down.

Five minutes.

"Prepare to engage jump engines, Pilot," Pacheco said.

"Yes, Admiral," came the woman's reply.

"Power up pulse cannons," said Pacheco to the weapons officer.

His neck ached with tension. He rubbed it. He breathed in deeply before exhaling long and slow. "Ready, everyone."

The seconds ticked away on his interface display. The air seemed syrupy and hard to breathe. The stress in the room pressed down.

The battle that could unlock a future of peace for galactic civilization was about to begin.

Pacheco's display read zero.

"Jump."

13

———

The *Thylacine* was ready to starjump across the galaxy to the remaining Shadow-controlled region. As she sat on the ship's bridge for the countdown to the jump, Jas was reminded of the fact that the ship would pass momentarily through the Void on its journey. She had learned that fact during her myth run at Ganymede Station. The Paths had told her that glimpses of the starships of the physical universe dipping into the Void while they starjumped had enticed the Shadows to devise a method to cross the barrier and find out more about this plane that was new to them.

Up until then, no one had known or even guessed the Shadows' motivation for their invasion, but the knowledge didn't seem to matter. It wasn't as if the sentient species of the galaxy could give up using starjump technology. Traveling the vast distances across space would be impossible without it. The energy required to power transgalactic gateways was so great that transporting large numbers of people or large amounts of goods wasn't economically viable. Jas wondered if traveling via gateway also meant stepping briefly into the Void.

It was unfortunate that the jump drive had resulted in enticing the Shadows to enter the galaxy, but she had no compassion or sympathy for the creatures. They were responsible for the deaths of millions, and one man in particular whose loss she would never recover from. She could never forgive what the Shadows had done, and she relished this opportunity to grind them to dust beneath her heel.

They jumped.

Starjumping such a large distance always left everyone disoriented for a moment. Jas blinked as the bridge came into focus around her.

A holo popped up. As Pacheco had told her, a large Shadow ship was in the vicinity. It was bigger than the *Thylacine,* but they had the element of surprise. With a grim smile, Jas imagined the reactions of the Shadow captain and his crew when they registered the *Thylacine's* presence, heavily armed and force field up.

"Pulse cannons at the ready," Jas said. "Fire."

A battery of pulses flew from the *Thylacine's* cannons, arcing across space, toward the Shadow ship. The first arrived before the ship's force field was fully employed, and the holo displayed a satisfying splash of light directly across its hull. The following pulses hit soon after, spreading out across the force field and dissipating into space.

"Second degree hull damage on the enemy ship, Commander," Trimborn said, his gaze intent on his console.

Score one to the *Thylacine.* The following battle might be long and hard until they finally subdued the enemy vessel, but they already had an advantage.

The return pulses weren't slow in coming, but the *Thylacine's* force field shrugged them off.

Jas leaned forward in her seat to look at the holo of the Shadow ship more closely. "Trimborn, is that a—"

"Class three destroyer, ma'am," the first officer replied. "Unity ship."

He looked up from his screen to give her a wry smile. Class three destroyers had been phased out of production because they had a notorious weakness: their new model, RaptorY engines were prone to exploding if the surrounding hull were breached, and the explosion would take out the entire ship.

Jas's face registered grim satisfaction. "Kennewell, take us aft of that ship."

"Yes, Commander."

The pilot fired the *Thylacine's* more trustworthy RaptorXs, and maneuvered the vessel on a course to bring them behind the Shadow ship.

The Shadow in command seemed to guess their intent, for the enemy ship began to swing around in response to the *Thylacine's* maneuver.

"Ha," Jas said, slapping her knee. "Looks like we're in for a game of cat and mouse. Kennewell, get us behind that ship, whatever it takes. Trimborn, maintain full pulse barrage." While it was under sustained attack, the ship wouldn't be able to build the power to jump.

Abrupt acceleration crushed Jas into her seat as Kennewell powered the *Thylacine* on a vertical trajectory. The officers who were standing bent at the knees and gripped their consoles. A violent lurch of the ship threw everyone to the right as the holo displayed their rapidly moving vessel speeding closer to the Shadow ship.

"There it goes," Trimborn said, remarking on the Shadow ship's rapid descent, almost off the display.

"I'm after it," Kennewell said, and Jas was airborne for a moment as the *Thylacine* plunged toward the enemy vessel. Bolts of light were passing between the two ships as pulse after pulse shot out of them.

"Force field eighty percent," Trimborn said. The *Thylacine's* power reserves were beginning to drain. Jas bit her lip. If they could last longer than the enemy vessel, they'd win in the end, providing—

"Ah, krat," Jas said, forgetting her dignity as a commander for a moment as sparks of light flowed from the Shadow ship. The enemy hadn't been slow in deploying its fighter ships. And it appeared to have over a hundred of them.

"Direct pulses at those ships, Trimborn," Jas said, hoping to take out enough to force them to retreat.

The *Thylacine's* pulses changed direction and began cutting through the cloud of fighters. But the pulses could only take out a handful at a time before disappearing into space. Meanwhile, the enemy ship's pulses rained down on the *Thylacine*. The force field was holding for the time being, but the ship shuddered and shook as the pulses impacted.

"Force field forty-six percent," Trimborn said.

Kennewell was doing her utmost to bring the *Thylacine* to the rear of the Shadow ship, but the enemy also clearly had a pilot who was excellent at playing the mouse.

"Force field thirty-five percent," said Trimborn.

With a heavy heart, Jas spoke into her comm, "Squadron Leader, scramble all fighters." Lifting her head, she said, "Trimborn, return pulse fire to the enemy ship."

Pulses wouldn't stop the enemy's fighter ships, and no

matter how fast Kennewell piloted the *Thylacine*, the large ship was no match for their speed or maneuverability. They would soon be close enough to fire at her.

The *Thylacine's* fighters erupted from her launch bay. A collective gasp sounded on the bridge as a pulse from the Shadow ship cut a swathe through its own fighter ships, destroying the sparks like a jet of water on a fire. The Shadows were killing their own pilots to target the *Thylacine's*.

Sayen turned a white, stricken face to Jas.

"Looks like they're prepared to do anything to win this battle," Jas said grimly.

The Shadow fighter ships were drawing nearer, and the *Thylacine's* moved to engage with them. Another pulse flew from the Shadow ship, wiping out not only Shadow fighter ships, but the *Thylacine's* too.

"What the krat are they doing?" Trimborn burst out. "What's the point of sending out fighters just to destroy them?"

"As long as a few get through," Jas said, "and none of ours survive, they could cause us some serious damage. And if we go after the fighters directly, that prevents us from targeting their ship."

She bit the side of her thumb and stared at the holo.

She barked, "Kennewell, for krat's sake, get us below that ship." The *Thylacine* would draw some of the Shadow ship's fire. But as they moved, the Shadow's faster fighter planes were right on their tail.

"Commander," Sayen said. "What if we jump?"

Jump? They couldn't do that. It would mean leaving their fighters behind in the hands of the enemy. Unless she meant...

"Can we do that, S—Navigator?" Jas asked.

"It'll be close," Sayen replied, "but as long as our fighters stay at the fore, they should be protected."

"Do it," Jas said. "Trimborn, cut pulses. We're going to jump."

"Jump, ma'am?" the first officer asked.

"Jump engines powering, Commander," Kennewell said.

Sayen bent over her interface, rapidly calculating the jump.

"Prepare for full pulse barrage the second we jump," Jas said. "No force field."

Kennewell was watching Sayen, waiting for the coordinates. Without lifting her head, Sayen raised a hand and pointed at the pilot.

But she shook her head. "Still waiting on the engines."

Without their pulses targeting those incoming from the Shadows, the *Thylacine* was taking a brutal beating once more. On the holo, their ship was a ball of light as the pulses spread out across her force field. The Shadow fighters had also broken through the defense laid down by the *Thylacine's* pilots.

"Force field eighteen percent," Trimborn said. "Damage to hull, port, and starboard."

Jas prayed her squadron leader would notice the *Thylacine* was building to a jump and guess her intention. Her gaze was fixed on those tiny flecks of light that represented the lives of more than eighty women and men. If their fighters were too close when they jumped, they would be killed. One or two lingered in the unsafe zone. *Come on. Move.*

"Force field seven percent."

"Get out of the way," Jas exclaimed, hitting her arm rest.

As if in response, the *Thylacine's* fighter ships that were in danger began to peel away, fleeing the vicinity like fish escaping a shark's mouth.

"Jumping in fifteen seconds," Kennewell said.

The officers dropped into their seats and fastened their harnesses.

"Five seconds," said Kennewell.

"Remember that barrage, Trimborn," Jas said. "Don't waste time on the force field."

"Yes, ma'am," the first officer said, and then they jumped.

The *Thylacine* reappeared less than a heartbeat later right behind the Shadow ship. Trimborn unleashed the full might of her pulse cannons on one spot—the site of the RaptorY engines. The Shadow ship's force field was still strong, but not strong enough to protect the ship from the concentrated power of the *Thylacine*. The captain also took too long to realize what was happening.

A single pulse sped from the enemy ship in their direction before its force field collapsed. The *Thylacine's* next attack penetrated the hull, hitting both RaptorY engines. As soon as the breach appeared, without waiting for the order, Kennewell pulled the *Thylacine* violently away, throwing everyone on the bridge forward.

Another pulse from the Shadow ship and the blast of its explosion hit the *Thylacine,* throwing it backward even faster. Kennewell didn't slow the ship down until they were safely beyond the explosion zone.

"Hull breach," Trimborn said. "Losing atmosphere decks two and three. And we're on fire."

They'd sustained some damage, but they'd done it. The Shadow ship was nothing but scattered debris.

"Direct comm to Admiral Pacheco," Jas said.

The comm officer pressed his console and spoke into his

mic. He nodded and took off his earpiece before holding it out to Jas. She strode over, held the earpiece to one ear and spoke into the mic.

"Mission successful, Admiral. The Shadow ship's destroyed."

"Then get over here," came Pacheco's reply. "The *Camaradon* needs you."

14

T he *Thylacine's* engines began building to starjump again. Jas spoke to the repair crews who were sealing the hull breech, telling them they had three minutes to get everyone behind sealed bulkheads. As she spoke, her eyes were on the holo. The surviving fighter pilots were streaming back to the safety of the *Thylacine's* launch bay, though the remaining Shadow fighters were engaging them in dog fights.

With their mother ship gone, they were as good as dead. They had nothing to lose. And if Jas left without them, her fighters were in nearly the same predicament, though if the *Thylacine* made it through, they would return to search for them.

Sayen was busy calculating their next jump from the coordinates given by the *Camaradon*. Jas wondered what the problem was. The Unity's fleet ship had never been beaten in battle. She had never even had her hull breached, as far as Jas was aware. And Pacheco knew what he was doing when it came to space battles. Maybe their intelligence had underestimated the enemy's firepower.

"Trimborn," Jas said, "what power capacity are we at?"

"After this jump," he replied, "I estimate seventy-three percent."

Not too bad, but not great either. Not for entering another intense engagement. Pacheco knew that, yet he'd still asked them to come. Things had to be bad.

"Sending coordinates," Sayen said.

"Got them," said Kennewell. "Engine three minutes from jump, Commander."

Jas gripped her arm rests and stared down at the list of pilots' names ever present on her screen. The dots were missing from a large percentage, and as she watched, one of the lights wavered and went out. Looking up at the holo, she saw the fighter vessels approaching, dogged by fire from the Shadow fighters.

"Trimborn," she said, "can you aim a pulse at those Shadow vessels without risking hitting our own ships?"

He frowned over his console for a moment before replying, "Yes, ma'am."

"It will delay our jump a few seconds, Commander," the comm officer said.

Kennewell scowled at him.

"I'm aware of that," said Jas. "Do it." She watched as the short pulse from the *Thylacine* obliterated the tail end of the Shadow fighters. The *Thylacine's* fighters were already arriving at the ship and entering the launch bay. The remaining pilots fought off the Shadows still chasing them.

"Jumping in one minute," Kennewell said.

Their fighters were going to make it. Jas checked with the repair crew that everyone was in a place of safety, and she told the rest of the ship to get to their jumpseats. She comm'd the Squadron Leader to tell his pilots to remain aboard their vessels for the jump.

Jas leaned back in her seat and passed a hand over her eyes. The adrenaline from the battle was fading, leaving behind a deep fatigue. She felt like she could sleep for a month. *Just one last effort*, she told herself. Just one last fight, then it would all be over. Sayen could return to Earth and her brother, Toirien could be reunited with her daughters, and Pacheco could find someone else to moon over.

What she would do, she didn't know, but neither did she care.

"Here we go," Kennewell said, and Jas felt the familiar falling sensation.

"Krat, would you look at that," exclaimed Trimborn as the holo of the battle scene flickered to life.

The *Thylacine* had appeared to one side of a flurry of pulse fire. Pacheco had brought them right into battle, and it soon became obvious why. The *Camaradon* was under severe attack.

Jas's heart froze at the sight. A mere few hundred thousand kilometers from the *Camaradon* was a ship bigger than any she'd ever seen. It dwarfed the massive Unity ship like a planet did a moon. The ship's make was also entirely unfamiliar.

Her mind flew back to the *Thylacine's* battle with the unfamiliar Shadow ships. The Shadows *had* been building their own ships. They'd moved on from using their victims' knowledge and skills and begun to innovate and create. Had the ships Jas encountered been mere test vessels for the technology of this new, gargantuan ship?

"Attack that ship," she shouted, leaping out of her seat. "Full pulses."

Her hand rose to her mouth. Had they been tricked? Had the entire battle been the Shadows' idea? Had the

Camaradon and the other Unity Alliance vessels been lured into a trap?

Her eyes rose to the holo of the Shadow ship that overhung the bridge. She scanned the vessel for any familiarities —sensor arrays, drive assemblies, cannons—anything that could give her a handle on what they were dealing with. But the ship was a mystery to her. Even its firepower was different. A long stream of energy burst from it, not the familiar bolts of pulses.

The *Camaradon* was being raked by this raw firepower, and its own barrage of pulses were being trapped and eradicated by the wavering energy beam before they could even hit the Shadow ship.

As they watched, more Unity Alliance ships blinked into existence, called to the *Camaradon's* aid, yet they looked like fleas hopping around a dog.

The *Thylacine's* pulses attracted the attention of the energy beam. It flicked toward them, and the pulses were gone. The familiar burst and dissipation of charged particles was missing, however. Had the beam absorbed the energy? Were the *Camaradon's* pulses being converted and returned to it as firepower?

"Stop firing all pulses," Jas said. "Comm the Admiral."

"I can't, ma'am," the comm officer said. "Our comms are being scrambled. Everything that leaves or enters our system."

Krat. Jas got up and went over to the holo. The behemoth Shadow ship dominated the display but Unity Alliance ships surrounded it on all sides. The number of ships indicated that the UA had been successful in most of their individual battles, but that wouldn't mean anything if they lost the *Camaradon.*

The Shadow ship was bigger and the Shadow's technology was better, but the UA had to win this fight. If they didn't the enemy would begin to push back, retaking the planets that had been cleaned of their presence, infiltrating new worlds. All the battles of the previous five years, all the lives that had been lost would have been for nothing.

But how could they defeat the Shadow's devastating ray?

As Jas watched the holo, tiny sparks began to stream from the belly of the *Camaradon*. Pacheco had launched his fighter ships, sending individual women and men in their tiny craft against that terrifying beam of light that was possibly being fed by pulses from the UA side.

But Pacheco had the right idea. If pulses couldn't break through the Shadow ship's defenses, the only chance the UA had of destroying the ship was the force field-penetrating, low-energy fire of the fighters. If they could wreck whatever it was that was creating that ray, the *Camaradon* and the UA still stood a chance.

Jas and everyone else on the bridge held their breath as the tiny sparks representing the brave *Camaradon* pilots neared the Shadow ship. The enemy's beam was still flickering over the battleship like electricity in a Van de Graff generator. Jas desperately hoped that the fighters would escape the beam, but as the sparks swooped nearer, forks of light split from the ray and took out the leading ships.

The remaining fighters took evasive action, diverting from a direct course toward the Shadow ship and splitting into different flight paths. But no matter what course the pilots took, the beam seemed to sense their presence, sending out long trails of light that split from the central ray.

All around the bridge something between a gasp and a groan sounded. It was a massacre. The pilots were going like lambs to the slaughter. They couldn't evade the dreadful ray, and they couldn't get close enough to the Shadow ship to employ their firepower.

There was nothing, nothing anyone could do to protect them or fight back.

Suddenly, the Shadow's beam broke through the *Camaradon*'s force field and hit the hull around one of its starjump engines. Jas's chest constricted. If the ray broke through the hull, the ship would be incapacitated, unable to jump. If it couldn't escape, it would be destroyed, along with the two thousand or more lives aboard.

Jump, for krat's sake. Jump. Yet she knew jumping was impossible for the *Camaradon* now. Her hands were fists.

"What should we do, ma'am?" Trimborn asked. His tone caused Jas to turn to look at him. The man's usually sanguine expression had turned to fear. He was reading the next steps of the battle the same as she was.

The *Camaradon* was halfway to being lost. Pacheco had been expending all the ship's power on pulses and her force field. He couldn't afford to drop what remained of the force field either, or it would mean immediate annihilation. It would take ages for the ship to build the power to jump, and meanwhile the Shadow's beam was targeting the very engines that might save it.

Jas wouldn't fire at the Shadow ship—that only seemed to help it. There was nothing they could do. Her first responsibility was to her crew.

"Kennewell, prepare to jump."

"Yes, Commander."

"Jas," Sayen exclaimed, her face stricken, but there was no time to explain.

It would take several minutes for the *Thylacine* to generate jump power. When the engines were at maximum capacity, they could remain in that state for several more minutes. At the current state of the battle, that should be long enough to do something to help if the opportunity arose. Though the longer they waited before expending the massive amounts of energy, the more danger they were in of simply exploding.

"Navigator," Jas said, "plot a course for as far away from here as we can go."

Sayen nodded, understanding that Jas was going to wait until the last possible second before they jumped, requiring the *Thylacine's* engines to top out their power.

How long would it take before Pacheco realized the battle was already over?

"Open launch bay doors," Jas said, then spoke into her comm. "Squadron Leader, maneuver all fighter ships to the back of the launch bay. Prepare to receive survivors."

"Yes, ma'am." The man's tone was relieved.

Trimborn's sharp intake of breath caused her to look up. Light flared blindingly from the holo of the *Camaradon*. The Shadows' beam had broken through the hull of one of its jump engines and released the energy Pacheco had been building to jump.

That was it. He had to abandon ship now. Around the holo of the Shadow ship, UA vessels began to wink out of existence, their captains and commanders retreating before the dreadful ray was turned on them.

Come on, Pacheco. Save your crew.

If only the Shadow ship wasn't scrambling their comms, Jas could have ordered the remaining *Camaradon* fighters to retreat to the *Thylacine*. Some were returning to their stricken ship, some were continuing to brave the terrifying ray. Jas wished they'd see sense and give up their hopeless attack.

Pacheco, come on.

"Ready to jump, Commander," Kennewell said.

Jas's gaze frantically searched the belly of the *Camaradon*. Any evacuees needed to leave immediately if they were to reach the *Thylacine* before she would have to jump. She exhaled. A few specks had appeared. Fighters that Pacheco must have told to turn around when they arrived. They headed in the direction of UA ships, but some were jumping before they could reach them.

Thankfully, some were heading for the *Thylacine*.

Larger specks appeared. The evac ships. These held one hundred. Some of the crew were getting away, but Jas thought it would take longer than the *Camaradon* had to launch them all.

As an evac flew from the *Camaradon's* belly, it attracted the notice of the Shadow's beam. A lick of lightning, and one hundred lives were lost. Somewhere on the bridge, a voice cried out.

"Ma'am," Kennewell said, "the jump engines are becoming unstable."

Jas didn't reply. She was biting the edge of her thumb. Blood was running down her hand to her wrist.

"Commander," Kennewell said.

Jas opened her mouth to answer, but at that moment another evac ship appeared and began to streak toward the *Thylacine*, one of the few UA ships remaining in the vicinity.

"Squadron Leader," Jas said into her comm. "An evac's on its way to us. Tell me the second it arrives."

Everyone on the bridge was frozen, transfixed as the evac drew swiftly closer.

"Ma'am," Kennewell said, a note of desperation in her voice.

Jas ignored her.

"Commander," Trimborn exclaimed, "the *Camaradon's* going to blow."

Jas ignored him too.

The Squadron Leader's voice sounded from her comm. "Evac ship's aboard, ma'am. Launch bay doors closed."

"Jump."

15

———

Sayen was helping with the survivors from the *Camaradon*. Most were in shock, but very few were injured. The first evac ship had been filled with the injured. The evac ship that the Shadows' beam had destroyed.

Twelve fighter pilots had made it to the safety of the *Thylacine's* launch bay. Along with the hundred of the *Camaradon's* crew who had made it to the evac ship that made one hundred and twelve. One hundred and twelve out of two thousand. Sayen hoped that other evac ships had reached UA vessels before they jumped. Jas had said they would return to the battle scene in an hour to look for survivors. Fighter ships had twenty-four hours of life support. There was a slim chance that some pilots were still out there, or even an evac ship or two that had escaped the Shadows' notice.

It was a slim hope, but Sayen clung to it as she walked among the survivors, who were sitting and standing in groups in the launch bay: technicians, engineers, troops, and general maintenance staff. Sayen handed out blankets and energy drinks, which were accepted with shaking hands. Most of the survivors were silent, others were crying.

She didn't see Pacheco until she was nearly upon him. He was sitting by himself, looking the most shocked of all.

"Admiral," Sayen said, holding out a drink she'd opened. "Are you okay, sir?"

He looked from the drink to her face for a moment as if not hearing or understanding what she'd said, then recognition dawned in his eyes.

"Navigator Lee," he replied, his voice choked. "Thank you." He took the drink. "Is Commander Harrington on the bridge?"

"Yes, sir."

"Thanks." He stood up unsteadily and walked away, his hand drooping, spilling his drink in a trail along the floor. Sayen went after him, concerned about his state. He stopped and turned to her. "She made me leave, you know."

"Sir?" Sayen asked.

"The Fleet Admiral. I wanted to stay. A captain should go down with his ship. I was going to stay. But she made me leave. She told me there was nothing I could have done. It was false intelligence. A trap to take out our best ship. The Shadows will make their move now. They've begun to push back. I have to help coordinate our response."

"Yes, sir."

"You do understand? I had to leave. I didn't want to abandon my ship."

"Yes, sir. I understand completely."

The admiral nodded to himself. "Don't worry. I know the way." He left the launch bay.

Others of the *Thylacine's* crew had also come to the bay to help with the survivors, and to search for family members and loved ones. These latter went from group to group asking for news. Sometimes the news wasn't what they wanted to hear, such as that the person they were looking for had been injured and on the first evac ship. Crew members were hugging and crying.

Sayen recognized a ginger-haired woman, and she went over to see her.

"Toirien," she said. "Jas told me you were aboard."

"Umm...," Toirien replied, her freckled face turning pink.

"I'm Sayen Lee. From the *Galathea*."

"Oh, right. Hi," Toirien replied, in a tone that said she still didn't know who this strange woman was.

"Navigator Lee. Do you remember?"

"Oh," exclaimed Toirien. "I remember. You were the one in stasis in the sick bay while we were trapped on the Shadow planet."

"Yes, that was me. But I was also the ship's navigator for the mission."

Toirien shook her head. "I'm sorry. I didn't really take any notice of who was who aboard the ship. I mostly kept my head down and got on with my job then. I was fighting my demons."

"Demons?"

"Never mind." Toirien held out a hand and they shook. "It's good to meet you finally. I just wish it was in better circumstances. I came here to look for my daughter. She was an engineer aboard the *Camaradon*, but someone just told me she was transferred to another ship before the battle. Now I don't know where she is."

"I'm sorry," Sayen said, "I hope she's okay. I hate to ask you this, but could you help me with something if you have time? I want to find berths for these people."

"It'd be my pleasure. The engines are ready to roll, and I

was starting to feel a little useless. I don't know how to help these people."

Sayen found Trimborn, who was inputting the survivors' details into the ship's system, and explained what she wanted to do.

"Be my guest," Trimborn said, handing her an interface. "That was next on my list. While you're doing that, I can organize people to help the doctor with triage and dispensing sedatives."

Sayen and Toirien searched the *Thylacine*'s system for spare berths or other potential sleeping accommodation and assigned the survivors to bunks. They would need somewhere to sleep after the doctor's sedatives began to take effect. A period of recovery was needed, though what would happen after, Sayen didn't know.

"Toirien," she said, "you got to know the commander quite well while you were on the Shadow planet, didn't you?"

"Yeah, pretty well. I like her, though she's got a tough side to her."

"Would you say she's changed a lot?"

"Krat, yes," Toirien exclaimed. "I don't know how she's still standing, to be honest. Never seen someone look so bad who wasn't sick in bed. If I didn't know better, I'd say she was on something."

"Really?" Sayen asked. "You think the commander might be on drugs?"

"No, that's not what I said. From the way she acted toward me on the *Galathea*...Sayen, I have to confess, I used to have a bad drug and alcohol habit, so I know what I'm talking about. What I said was, *if I didn't know better*. Jas Harrington hates drugs, and, anyway, she isn't the type to take them. She's no thrill seeker. But she looks just as exhausted and ill as if she were on something strong and had been for a long time. I should know. I used to mix with those people. I was one of those people."

"I think she looks bad too," Sayen said. "I'm worried about her, Toirien."

"It must be the stress of command that's wearing her out."

"No, I don't think it's that. Or at least, that isn't all of it. Jas used to be a strong person. All that's gone now. It's like she's only just holding on."

"Well, I don't want to add to our commander's troubles..." Toirien looked around and took Sayen's upper arm, pulling her into a quiet spot in the corridor outside the launch bay. "Talking of drugs, I think we may have a problem aboard this ship."

"Seriously?"

"As I said, I used to be in that scene, and I see all the signs. There's myth or something similar doing the rounds."

"Myth? But it's so expensive. How could ordinary Unity crew afford it?"

"I've no idea, but I swear there's some intense dealing going on. I think one of my engineers might be an addict, but I'm not sure. I don't want to formally accuse her. If I'm wrong, that kind of mud sticks."

Sayen ran a hand through her hair. Myth was the scourge of the galaxy. "Have you said anything to the commander?"

"I didn't want to burden her when I don't have any proof."

"Yeah, she has enough on her plate. Thanks for telling me. I'll mention it to her if I find the right moment."

"Okay." Toirien scanned the interface. "Hey, there's an empty bunk in this cabin."

Sayen filed away Toirien's tip about drugs aboard the ship. It was definitely not a good time to give Jas more to deal with. In an ironic kind of way, Sayen realized, it was good for Jas that the war wasn't over. She had a suspicion it was the only thing keeping her friend going right now.

16

P acheco was familiar with the layout of the *Thylacine*, but he'd gotten lost on his way to the bridge. He suddenly noticed he was wandering the corridors on the lower decks, which were empty and quiet.

Ever since abandoning the *Camaradon*, he'd felt light-headed. Everything around him seemed surreal. Images of the battle flashed constantly through his mind, making it hard for him to concentrate on his surroundings and what people said to him. They sounded like they were speaking to him through cotton wool or from a far distance.

He'd never lost a ship before.

He recalled the *Camaradon's* jump into the remaining Shadow-controlled sector of the galaxy and the discovery of the gigantic Shadow ship. Its sheer size had been impossible to grasp. His first officer had checked and rechecked the scanner readings.

A ship that large had never been built before in the history of the galaxy. Pacheco hadn't even thought it was possible to build a ship so big.

He had barely had time to register that it was real and

the scanners weren't lying before it unleashed its onslaught. The Shadow's terrible ray had tested the strength of the *Camaradon's* force field from the very moment it struck.

He stumbled over his own feet and fell against the passageway wall. He gripped it for support, shaking his head. But he couldn't shake the memory of the behemoth dominating the holo on the *Camaradon's* bridge, or of the fearful faces of his officers when they'd realized what they were up against.

The Unity Alliance had been too confident; too sure of its intelligence. Reports had said that the Shadow flagship was in the vicinity, and the reports had been correct. But they had completely underestimated the size of the craft. It had all been a ruse to trap the Unity Alliance into committing its best ship to an unwinnable battle.

Their final, decisive blow against the Shadows had turned into a crushing defeat.

Pacheco told himself he'd fought the best he could, but the words sounded empty in his head. His view of the *Thylacine's* passageway disappeared and was replaced by the sight of the *Camaradon* firing pulse after pulse at the Shadow ship, and the awful ray wiping them up as if they were mere annoyances, all the while pouring its dreadful energy at the *Camaradon's* force field.

In his mind, the rest of the fleet appeared after their battles once more, called to the *Camaradon's* aid. But their pulses were also useless against the enemy. The Shadow ship had never seemed to even weaken. Where the ship derived its power from, Pacheco couldn't understand. He wasn't a scientist, but he was sure that such amounts of energy were impossible to generate and expend so rapidly.

His legs shook and he dropped to his knees. He slumped against the bulkhead, his eyes closed, reliving the memory of the last, desperate measures before their inevitable defeat. He'd sent out the fighter ships in an all-but-doomed attempt to break through the Shadow ship's defenses. He relived the realization that the *Camaradon* would never generate the energy to jump unless its force field were turned off, and that it would mean a quick, fiery death for everyone aboard.

Yet if they couldn't jump, the *Camaradon* was lost.

The Camaradon was lost. Pacheco drew his hand down his face. It came away wet.

The Fleet Admiral had been the one who had given the command to abandon ship. Should it have been him? Had he insisted on fighting too long, when it was clearly hopeless? Had lives been lost needlessly because of him? He would never know. He also didn't know if it had been his false optimism that had made him keep the *Camaradon* fighting, thinking that, somehow, the battle would turn in their favor, or if it had been pure arrogance and stubbornness—an unwillingness to believe he could ever lose.

The flashing emergency lights and klaxon of the final minutes echoed in his mind. He saw the fighter pilots seeking refuge in other UA ships before they jumped. He recalled giving the order to evacuate the sick and injured first, and the horror as the Shadow ship annihilated their vessels. He relived the last desperate, hopeless rush to the evac ships, choosing probable over certain death.

His final memory was of the fleet admiral's insistence that he leave, telling him that the UA needed him if they were to fight back. Then came the sole moment of peaceful, dreamlike wonder as the fleet admiral had knelt down, and bowed her head. It had dissolved into hundreds of pieces, which floated gently in her helmet.

Somehow, Pacheco's recollection of that moment of

gentle death steadied his racing heart and whirling mind. Even in her last moments, the fleet admiral had held onto hope. As Pacheco understood it, she had entered the reproductive cycle of her species, and pieces of her could grow into a new Haidiren.

Would they survive the explosion and the cold and vacuum of deep space? Perhaps thousands or millions of years in the future landing on a watery planet and beginning to grow? Pacheco didn't know, and it didn't matter. The fact was, the fleet admiral had demonstrated that in the direst circumstances, hope can survive.

He blinked. He was back aboard the *Thylacine*. The empty passageway had come into focus around him. His hat lay upside down on the floor, having fallen off unnoticed. He picked it up and replaced it on his head before pushing himself to his feet.

With some effort, he concentrated on walking toward an elevator that led to the upper decks and the bridge. He needed to find Jas—Commander Harrington. He had to contact the ships that had survived as well as the Transgalactic Council. The *Camaradon* was lost, but that didn't mean the war was over.

The elevator doors opened as he approached. He told it where he wanted to go, and it sped upward. He took the opportunity to check his appearance in the shiny steel of the walls. He straightened his hat and smoothed his uniform.

The elevator doors opened. The passageways were busy there, near the bridge. He ducked across the crowded thoroughfare and went quickly to the nerve center of the ship, where Commander Harrington was sure to be.

His arrival on the bridge caused a minor stir.

"Admiral," Trimborn exclaimed as Pacheco entered and the bridge doors slid closed behind him.

Pacheco waited a moment while the man recovered from his apparent surprise and offered his salute. He returned it as the other officers on the deck offered theirs too.

Jas was standing. Despite everything that had happened in the last few hours, despite everything he'd been through, his heart still leapt at the sight of her.

She said, "Admiral, I'd like to speak with you in private if I may."

They went out into the busy passageway, and Jas took him to a quiet area.

"Where have you been, Pacheco?" she asked. "We had a ship-wide alert going. Navigator Lee said you left the launch bay over an hour ago. Where's your comm button?"

He looked down at the breast of his jacket. His button had been torn off in the crush aboard the evac vessel.

"I…I… needed to take some time to reflect. I didn't know I didn't have my comm."

Jas tilted her head and peered at him. "Are you okay?"

"I'm fine, Commander," he replied. She was acting like he was some kind of weakling. "Thank you for your concern."

"I'm glad to hear it, *Admiral*."

"Have you been in contact yet with the Transgalactic Council over the results of the battle?" he asked, ignoring her tone.

"Of course I have. They gave us coordinates to report at in twelve hours. We don't have any serious casualties that need better medical care than we have aboard ship."

Pacheco's mind replayed the destruction of the evac ship carrying the *Camaradon's* wounded.

"Pacheco?" Jas asked. "Pacheco?"

"What?" he snapped.

"I said, do you have any instructions for the *Thylacine?*

Are you sure you're all right? You zoned out for a moment there."

"Commander, I was present for the destruction of the flagship of the Unity Alliance fleet. I am not *all right*, but I expect I shall recover soon. Is that good enough for you?"

"Krat, take it easy, Pacheco," Jas said. "I was only trying to help. Maybe you should see the doctor."

Her words only irritated him further. He wasn't in need of any medication. He was stronger than that.

"And what's more," he said, "I want to make it clear that the fleet admiral *ordered* me to leave the ship."

Jas raised her hands in a gesture of conciliation. "Pacheco, no one thinks you're a coward. You did absolutely the right thing."

He ground his teeth. Though her words said the opposite, it sounded like she was accusing him of running away. A part of him knew he wasn't being reasonable, but that didn't change how he felt. He glared at her, and her expression grew angry in return.

Why did they always end up at loggerheads like this? He wondered. He remembered the years they'd worked together aboard the *Infineon*, after he'd been promoted to commander to replace Torbin.

"Pacheco," Jas barked. "You're zoning out again."

"I'm—"

"You're *not* fine. Go and see the doctor, or I'll have you confined because you're unfit to serve."

"You wouldn't—"

"Yes, I would. Go."

He clenched his jaw and glared, but the look in Jas's eye told him she wasn't going to back down. He spun around and stalked away. *Krat the woman.*

17

———

J as went back to the bridge and, ignoring the inquiring gazes that met her, flopped down into her seat. They'd lost. Just when she thought it would all be finally over, they'd lost. The prospect of the Shadow War continuing stretched out endlessly in front of her. She'd thought she could make it through to the end. Now, she wasn't so sure.

Everybody on the bridge was intent on their tasks, checking the *Thylacine's* systems for damage after the battle, programming diagnostics and repairs, making sure everything was shipshape. But was there any point? How would the Unity Alliance be able to defeat that monster Shadow ship?

The Shadows must have been building it for years, she realized. Safe from prying eyes within their stronghold, developing new materials and weapons and biding their time while the UA slowly drew closer.

As long as the ships it was battling were its own, the UA victory had seemed achievable. No one knew those ships better than those who had built them. They'd been perfectly prepared, exploiting their advantage of knowing exactly what the commandeered Shadow ships were capable of and what their weaknesses were.

But the beings from another dimension were far from dumb. They must have realized long ago what the outcome would be if they continued on the same path. They'd understood they needed to use a different tactic, and they'd chosen the correct one.

The devastation of losing the *Camaradon* was only the beginning. The Shadows had seen the success of their superior technology, and they wouldn't be slow to press on, reversing all the gains the UA had made, retaking the planets they'd lost, restarting stalled invasions.

Jas slumped forward and put her head in her hands. She wanted to fight the Shadows. She wanted her revenge for them taking away the only living man she would ever love, but she was at the end of her tether. She wished she were just an ensign again, or a security officer, so that someone else would bear the responsibilities that rested on her.

She felt so alone. Pacheco, annoying though he was at times, had been someone to rely upon, but even he seemed to have lost it.

"Commander," said a voice.

Jas looked up. It was Kennewell.

"I was wondering when we were going to return to look for survivors," she said in a small voice.

Krat. Jas had been planning to return to the scene of the battle to check for fighter pilots who hadn't made it to a ship.

"What's the time?" she asked the bridge. When someone told her, she exploded.

"Why didn't any of you say anything before? Are you all kratting idiots? What's wrong with you? Do I have to spell every last thing out to you people? Sayen, plot the coordinates to put us a safe distance from the scene of the battle. Can you figure that out? Kennewell, prepare to jump."

Sayen was staring at her, open-mouthed. Jas glared, and the navigator swung around in her seat to her console. Kennewell began hastily pressing her controls. The rest of the officers on the bridge ducked their heads and focused more intently on their screens.

Jas slumped back in her seat and stared ahead, unseeing, hoping the war would end soon, one way or another. For her, it was already over.

18

───────

Sayen's coordinates put the *Thylacine* at the limit of scanner range from the scene of the battle. The limit of Unity Alliance scanner range, anyway. Sayen hoped that the Shadow ship, if it remained in the vicinity, didn't possess superior scanners as well.

As a precaution, the first thing they did upon arrival was to throw up a maximum power force field.

"I'm not picking up anything besides residual heat from the battle, Commander," Trimborn said, "and a lot of debris. The *Camaradon* blew to tiny pieces."

Jas sighed and rubbed her eyes. "No life signs?"

Trimborn expanded something on his screen, pulling it wider with his fingertips. "Nothing at all, ma'am."

"Take us in, Pilot," Jas said. "Slowly."

She looked awful. Sayen could now see what Toirien had meant when she'd said that her friend looked like she was on something. It wasn't only that Jas had lost weight, she looked unhealthy and weak. In all the time Sayen had known her, no matter how hard things had been, or even when people close to them had died, Jas had never looked as bad as she did right then. She looked like she'd given up on life.

She didn't seem to be despairing; it was more that there was an entire absence of emotion in her eyes. And what was worse, Sayen didn't know what she could do to help her old friend.

"Picking up a ship," Trimborn blurted. "It's just jumped in, ma'am."

Sayen's heart seized up. Had the Shadow ship returned to trap them?

"Ma'am, it's the *Vespira*. She's hailing us," the comm officer said.

"Thank krat for that," said Trimborn, just loud enough for Sayen to hear.

Jas had a short conversation with the captain of the *Vespira*. They agreed to divide the battle area into quadrants and search independently for any signs of life among the debris. It would reduce the time spent searching and also the time any survivors had to wait to be picked up. The battle had been fought far from any star systems, so at least there were no planets to search.

The mood on the bridge was somber as the *Thylacine* undertook its slow, sweeping scans of the scene of the battle. The embedded chips everyone wore didn't emit a signal a significant distance in deep space terms because their energy came from the wearer's metabolism. That meant that the chips stopped emitting a day or so after the wearer died. This had seemed cruel to Sayen when she first learned of it, but she later understood that recovering the bodies of dead crew only to then give them a space burial was seen as frivolous by the Unity.

"I can see one," Trimborn exclaimed.

"You mean you've picked up a signal?" Jas asked tiredly.

"Yes, we've got a live one. It's a fighter pilot. Sending coordinates, Kennewell."

The pilot eased the *Thylacine* closer to the stranded fighter ship, which was floating without power.

Sayen knew the procedure from rescue operations she'd taken part in previously. Another fighter would be sent out to either connect to the disabled vessel, or, if that wasn't possible, to grapple it into the launch bay. Then it was just a matter of retrieving the wounded pilot, hopefully without having to cut him or her from the wreckage.

Sayen turned to read Jas's expression. *She* hadn't entirely given up on finding Carl one day, but it looked as though Jas had. Her face was blank as she looked down at the interface screen on her armrest.

As soon as the *Thylacine* was near the shipwrecked pilot, Jas dispatched Squadron Leader Correia to bring the person in. Everyone on the bridge waited tensely while the rescue operation took place. The only information they had was the holo on Correia's and the stranded fighter ship, which didn't show them much. Trimborn gave regular updates on the signal from the pilot's chip. It gave only minimal information: heart rate, blood pressure, and oxygen saturation of the pilot's blood were all they knew of her or his physical state until the squadron leader made contact.

Jas had a direct comm with Correia, and the rest of the bridge couldn't hear what he said. They knew, however, when a message came through because Jas screwed up her face. The news wasn't good.

"Still in the land of the living, though?" she asked. When she heard the reply, she nodded, then spoke to the doctor, telling him to go to the launch bay to be on hand when the injured pilot was brought in.

Telling Trimborn to continue to scan for more survivors,

Jas stood up to leave the bridge. Knowing she wouldn't be needed for a while—Kennewell could map the sweep by herself—Sayen jumped up and went after her.

She trotted along the ship's passageway to catch up to her long-legged friend.

"Do you know who the pilot is?" she asked when she drew level.

Jas shook her head. "The name isn't on my manifest. Must be from another ship."

"Is he in a bad way?" Sayen asked.

"Pretty bad. Burned up and unconscious, Correia said."

"Krat," Sayen muttered. "Are you going to see him brought in?"

Jas nodded.

"I guess if the doctor can't treat him here, we'll have to jump to Unity medical facilities right away."

"Yeah," Jas replied. "That's not why I'm going down to the bay, though."

"Isn't it? Why are you then?"

Jas gave her an inscrutable look and didn't reply.

They arrived at the launch bay just as the doctor was bringing the patient out. Sayen couldn't make out the pilot's face, he was so badly burned. It was a miracle he was still alive. The doctor had put the patient on a life-support gurney and, along with Correia, he was pushing it toward them. A terrible smell of burned flesh hung in the air.

"Excuse me, Commander," the doctor said. "I must get this person to the sick bay immediately."

"Wait a moment, Doctor," said Jas. "Did you scan him?"

"No, of course not. No time. I can go through the formalities later."

He tried to push the gurney around Jas, who was in the

center of the passageway. She put a hand on the plexiglass lid, stopping the gurney dead.

"Scan your patient now, Doctor," Jas said.

The man tutted, but he comm'd a medic to bring over a Shadow scanner. "It's a waste of time, in my opinion, Commander. What are the chances of the Shadows burning up one of their own in an attempt to infiltrate our ranks?"

Jas folded her arms and looked at him implacably.

When the medic with the scanner arrived, the doctor opened the plexiglass lid. The sickening smell intensified. Sayen put a hand over her nose and mouth, though it made little difference. The doctor passed the scanner up and down the prone patient. Without looking at it, he lifted the scanner and held it toward Jas, display side facing her.

"Do you see?" he asked.

The display read: *Shadow Detected.*

Jas turned the scanner toward the doctor so that he could read it. As he saw the result, he turned pale. "I, er... " he stammered. Correia took a step backward and stared at the burned pilot in disbelief.

The terrible burnt smell had already made Sayen nauseated. At this latest revelation, she clenched her teeth and swallowed saliva to prevent herself from vomiting.

It had been another trap. The Shadow ship had vacated the vicinity, but they had left behind injured 'survivors' as plants to infiltrate the UA ships. What wouldn't they stoop to? Sayen wondered. Jas must have guessed the doctor would be too caught up in saving his patient to remember, or bother, to follow protocol and scan him.

"Airlock it," Jas said. She stood against the bulkhead and spoke into her comm. "Patch me through to the captain of the *Vespira.*"

The doctor was staring down at his blackened patient as Jas talked to the *Vespira's* captain.

"I can't believe it," he said. "How could they do such a thing?"

"I don't know," Sayen replied. "They used to be so similar to their victims, we couldn't tell them apart. But this, this is something beyond regular cruelty."

When the doctor still seemed to be frozen in disbelief, she added, "You'd better do as the commander said."

The doctor's head hung low. He flicked off the switches to the machines on the life support gurney. The equipment and screens turned silent and dark. Together, he and Correia pushed the gurney along the passageway until they came to an airlock. Sayen keyed in the code to open the inner door, and the doctor lifted the Shadow in his arms, still wrapped in a sheet. He went into the airlock and lay the creature almost gently on the deck before returning.

Sayen sealed the door. She started the sequence to open the outer lock. Figures counted down in the display. She didn't want to look, but somehow she wasn't able to take her eyes off the burned Shadow that lay unconscious through the airlock window. Had it suffered when they'd burned it? Had it volunteered or agreed to the deceit, or had it been coerced?

The display reached zero, and the outer doors opened. At the sound or sudden loss of temperature and atmosphere, the Shadow stirred. Horror rising up in her throat, Sayen saw its eyes flick open. Then it was gone, swept into space, the sheet trailing behind it.

19

J as went to the meeting at the Transgalactic Council like she was on autopilot. Nothing mattered anymore. She felt like a machine, going through the motions for as long as the war lasted.

Pacheco was also there. He seemed to have recovered a little from the loss of the *Camaradon*. His eyes no longer had a distracted look, and he was as smartly dressed as ever. He was seated with the other seven admirals and two fleet admirals. The large room was packed full of Unity Alliance commanders and captains. Everyone had been scanned twice by separate, randomly picked personnel before entering, and as always, the meeting room was proofed against any kind of surveillance.

Still, Jas couldn't help but wonder if somehow the Shadows had slipped in an informant. Not a Shadow, but someone who had gone over to their side, perhaps on the promise that they and theirs would not be harmed.

The golden insectoid alien who was the current head of the Council—Jas had heard that it was an unelected position, conferred by a lottery system among the qualified candidates—addressed the room.

"Fleet admirals, admirals, captains, and commanders of the Unity Alliance, I had hoped to have been greeting you in more joyful circumstances. I had mistakenly predicted that our most recent battle with the Shadows was to have been our last. Sadly, we now know that was a false hope.

"Our intelligence reports were not entirely incorrect, but they left out important information. The Shadows drew us into a trap, resulting in the destruction of our most powerful starship. They removed our key instrument in the fight, and now it would seem that they have the advantage.

"For this reason, I would like to suggest a different tactic, which is to be the subject of this meeting. I would urge you not to spend time regrouping, building new vessels, and so on. This is probably what the Shadows expect us to do. But we have discovered that our former strategy was not effective. We must not pursue old tactics. We must try something new. And for that reason, I and the rest of the Council's leaders suggest we must fight back now. We must commit everything we have remaining at this moment. The longer we wait, the stronger the Shadows will become."

"But if we attack now," interrupted a fleet admiral, "what do we attack them with? We have nothing to withstand that monster ship. I've seen the vids of the destruction of the *Camaradon*. That ray they have is like nothing I've ever seen before. Going against it with our current weaponry would be little short of suicide."

"We have a saying among my kind," the golden councilor replied. "When you cannot be the strongest, be the smartest."

"It seems like the Shadows are the ones who have been the smartest so far," grumbled the fleet admiral.

Jas rested her chin on her hand and watched the councilor through half-lidded eyes. It had something up its sleeve.

"We have carefully studied the reports of Admiral Pacheco and the captains and commanders who were present at the defeat of the *Camaradon*," the golden alien went on. "We have detected a theme running between the lines of the reports. In fact, some of the reports overtly stated the observation. The ray the Shadows used so effectively seemed to draw some of its power from the pulses it encountered. We cannot be sure of this, but if it is true, this fact offers us hope."

"How? That makes things worse," said the fleet admiral. "If we're right about that, it only means we can't even fire at it without that energy being fired back at us."

"It would indeed be a hopeless situation if all we were able to do was fire at it," the golden councilor said. "But let us think laterally, just for a moment."

Jas had the impression the Transgalactic Council leader was vastly more intelligent than those assembled around it, and it was simplifying everything while trying not to sound like it was talking down to them.

It went on, "If this Shadow beam can in fact absorb the energy of the pulses it encounters, and then redirect that energy outward, that means the pulse power must be drawn into the Shadow weapon first. And if it takes in pulse energy, what else might it draw in?"

There was a moment of silence while they pondered the councilor's question. What could the Shadow ship take into its beam that could harm it? Then, Jas realized what the councilor meant.

"A bomb," she said.

"Precisely," said the councilor. "If we can disguise a

bomb as a pulse, and fire it at the Shadow ship, we could destroy it."

"What kind of bomb?" the fleet admiral asked. "If it absorbs energy, we can't increase the power of our pulses."

"Indeed not," the councilor said. "But we may be able to disguise an anti-matter bomb in a pulse. A poison pill, so to speak. If the beam absorbs anti-matter, the result would be quite spectacular, I believe."

"Do you have such a bomb?" the fleet admiral asked.

"No, but our scientists are working on it as we speak. They believe such a thing can be constructed, though it would be very unstable. No matter. For now, we must act as though the bomb will be ready in time for us to use it. We must find the Shadow ship and prepare for an assault."

The discussion went on for longer than an hour, but Jas sat back and let them argue it out. Some of the UA leaders saw the councilor's idea as outlandish and unrealistic, and were more in favor of a guerrilla warfare style of resistance, similar to what the Shadows had been doing for the majority of the war. Others agreed with the councilor that a single, final, decisive blow was required as soon as possible. They said that their people would rather die than live in servitude and fear.

But the anti-matter bomb was the better idea, Jas thought, and the majority eventually agreed to it.

As she left the meeting to return to the *Thylacine*, Pacheco caught up to her.

"I think we made the right decision, don't you?" he asked.

"Yeah, I guess so."

"You don't sound enthusiastic about the idea."

"I'm not enthusiastic about much these days. This war's been going on too long."

"I got the impression you weren't doing so well," Pacheco said. "I, er, wanted to thank you for making me see sense the other day. I went to the doctor. That post-battle shock isn't to be messed with. I didn't really believe how bad it was until I experienced it."

When Jas didn't reply, he went on, "You know, you might benefit from a visit to the doc yourself. It doesn't hurt to have a checkup. Talk things over, maybe."

She smiled wryly. "Giving me a taste of my own medicine, Pacheco?"

"Think of it as gentle advice from a concerned friend. I've accepted you're never going to feel about me the same way I feel about you, Jas. But that doesn't mean I've stopped caring about you."

For the first time in a long while, Jas was moved. Pacheco's concern touched her. She stopped and looked into his eyes. "Thanks, but there isn't anything the doctor or anyone else can do that's going to make me feel better. It is what it is."

Pacheco nodded. "Well, I'm going to be around to keep an eye on you anyway. Now the *Camaradon's* gone, I'm to berth aboard the *Thylacine*."

Jas's warmth toward the admiral cooled a little. In spite of what he'd said, she had the impression he still hadn't given up hope of something closer between them.

20

I t took the Transgalactic Council only ten days to locate the Shadow's flagship vessel, but their scientists took over six weeks to develop the anti-matter bomb. The idea for the technology wasn't new, and they'd already been working on a prototype when the battle had occurred, so they hadn't had to start from scratch. The greatest challenge, Jas heard, was to envelop the anti-matter in pulse energy for long enough after its manufacture for it to be fired and taken in by the Shadow weapon. Anti-matter was incredibly unstable.

Also, the UA couldn't simply create the bomb, jump to the Shadow ship's position, and fire it into the Shadow's beam. It would have to send a ship that was carrying the bomb-making equipment to attack the Shadow vessel. If the bomb wasn't fired in time from the ship where it was created, it would explode and destroy the ship. So, to disguise what it was doing and to protect the vessel that carried the bomb-making equipment the UA decided to launch a regular attack.

The *Thylacine*, as an average-sized destroyer of the Unity

fleet—and therefore unlikely to attract undue attention from the Shadow ship—drew the short straw. Jas's ship was to carry the bomb-making equipment and unleash what everyone hoped would be the final blow, destroying the gigantic Shadow ship.

Six weeks of preparation for the battle hadn't improved Jas's feelings of hopelessness and exhaustion. She'd been busy attending all the meetings and briefings as well as overseeing a full update of all the *Thylacine's* systems and equipment so that the ship was in tiptop shape. She'd also had to deal with a myth problem that Sayen had told her about. Somewhere along the line as they'd been releasing mythrin-bearing planets from Shadow control, the refined drug had gotten aboard. She'd ordered a thorough search of the ship, and screened every crew member, finding and dismissing several addicts. But even so, the time had seemed to pass slowly.

She was responsible for the *Thylacine's* crew and the ship's operation, Pacheco was responsible for the installation of the bomb-making equipment and the deployment of the bomb. That part of the plan was top secret.

Finally, the day before the battle arrived. Jas watched the officers as they went through their checks. A few supplementary crew members were arriving that evening, and Trimborn was responsible for settling them in.

When everything was completed, she left the bridge and returned to her cabin for an early night. As she went through the passageways, the atmosphere aboard the ship was quiet and tense. The anti-matter bomb was a secret, but the crew couldn't fail to have noticed the new equipment being brought aboard. Jas wondered if they had guessed that the *Thylacine* was playing a larger-than-usual role in the battle.

She changed into her unflattering, Unity-issue pajamas, catching sight of herself in her cabin's mirror. She turned away from her wan face and tired eyes and climbed into her bunk. She lay down on her back with one arm over her eyes and mentally went through the battle plan for the next day. She'd had so much trouble sleeping lately, she'd gotten into the habit of drinking to relax herself. But it was the night before a battle and she had to remain sober, even though it meant that sleep would be a long time coming.

A while later, as she was finally on the edge of drifting off, her door chimed. She removed her arm from her eyes and squinted at the clock. Who the krat could it be at that hour? Trimborn wouldn't dare wake her unless it was something serious. Or was it Pacheco? She hoped that pre-battle tension hadn't rekindled his feelings for her.

She thumbed the door comm. "Who is it?"

"Jas, it's me," said a voice. A voice that stopped her heart.

Or was it only that she was tired and on the edge of sleep? She couldn't believe it was who she thought she'd heard. "Who?" she asked again, a tremble in her voice.

"Jas, open up. I have to talk to you."

Was her mind playing tricks on her? If so, she didn't want to be seen in her bunk by a crew member. She didn't give a voice command from where she was, but turned on the cabin's half-light, got out of bed and padded over to the interface screen that would show her who was outside. She swallowed, and turned on the screen.

At first, she almost didn't recognize him. He was standing with one hand on the bulkhead next to the door, his head bowed. She couldn't see his face. His brown curls were gone, replaced by a cropped military cut peppered with strands of gray. He was thinner too. But it was him. It was Carl Lingiari. Her Carl.

As she watched, momentarily too shocked to move, he lifted a hand to press the door's comm button again, but before he made contact, she opened the door. He looked up. Their gazes met. The sound of her thumping heart rushed through her ears. She couldn't speak.

Carl had aged more than the five years that had passed since she'd last seen him. Lines were traced on his previously boyish features, but his warm, kind, deep brown eyes were the same.

"Is it okay if I come in?" he asked, looking a little anxious.

Responding automatically, she stepped back. Carl came into her cabin and she closed the door. She leaned back on it, catching her breath as if she'd been running.

For a moment, they looked at each other in silence. She reached out and touched his arm. She wanted to reassure herself that he was real. She was still unsure if she was dreaming. He was wearing an old, faded flight suit. The material was worn and soft, and she could feel the lean, hard muscles of his arm beneath it.

"Where have you been?" she whispered. "Where have you been all this time?"

"I've been fighting, of course," he replied. "Flying fighter ships, for years." He looked down. "Jas, I wanted to tell you I'm sorry for leaving you like that. When I volunteered, I never thought the war would take so long. I wanted to contact you, but with the ban on personal comms, it was impossible. I didn't even know you'd joined up until I heard about the commander of the new destroyer, the *Thylacine*. After that, I kept asking to be assigned to her, but it never happened until—"

She stepped forward and grabbed him into her arms. She held him close, her senses overwhelmed by the solid, physical presence of the person she'd yearned for for years, until that yearning had turned into only a wishful hope, and then only a sad memory, for what had seemed like forever.

He put his arms around her and drew her closer still. "I didn't know if you still would be glad to see me after I left you," he said, his breath warm on her neck. "I missed you."

"I'm not mad at you," she replied, drinking in his scent and the warmth and strength of his body against hers. "I missed you too." She closed her eyes and tilted her head backward. He kissed her. Tingles ran through her, down to her fingertips and toes. Once more, her heart raced like she'd been running. Her skin prickled with sweat.

They kissed deeply. She felt the muscles of his back slide under her hands as his lips left hers and descended to her neck. She drew in a breath at their passionate touch and the soft scrape of his stubble. Desire for him overwhelmed her. She reached to the top of his flight suit to unzip it. His hands went under her pajama top and moved up her bare back.

For the next couple of hours, they tried to make up for years of unmet needs and unfulfilled longing before they fell asleep in Jas's bunk, their limbs entangled.

21

———

At some point during the night, Jas woke. Elation filled her for a moment, then it was supplanted by fear that the previous evening had been a dream. She moved her hand and encountered a muscled chest. Carl was still beside her, warm and very, very real.

She turned on the cabin's half-light. Her lover was deeply asleep. One of his hands was tucked between their two bodies, and the other rested on her breast, rising and falling with her breathing. Running down his visible arm and the side of his body were long, silvered scars—burn scars. She traced them with a finger.

What had Carl been through in the years they'd been apart? He had always been lean, but now he looked positively gaunt. Barely a trace of fat softened the outline of the muscles in his arms, legs, chest, and stomach. His eyes were underscored with dark circles, and exhaustion lined his features.

What trials had he endured? How had he survived?

With a slight start, she saw his eyes were half open and he was watching her. Not so deeply asleep after all, then.

"Hey," she murmured.

"Hey." He shifted position and briefly kissed her lips.

"How'd you get these?" She stroked his scarred arm.

"It looks worse than it was. I got a bit too close to a Shadow ship. Took a hit. But it was okay. My ship's extinguishers kicked in in time. You've got a war wound yourself." He kissed her ravaged thumb.

"It must have been terrible," Jas said. "I've been so worried about you. I didn't think you could have survived this long—Oh, krat," she exclaimed, half sitting up.

"It's okay," Carl said. "I'm fine. I just haven't had a chance to get the scars fixed yet."

"No, it's not that. I forgot about the battle tomorrow. Carl, you can't go out there." She couldn't send him out with the rest of the *Thylacine's* pilots to face the Shadows again.

"I have to go, Jas," Carl said softly. "It's my job."

"No, I won't allow it. Not now that I've only just got you back. You've done enough. Years and years of flying those fighters and risking your life. I won't let you do it again."

He pulled her down onto the bunk and wrapped his arms around her. He spoke into her ear. "Jas, you can't protect me. It wouldn't be right. What about the other pilots? You can't put me before them."

"No," Jas said, tortured. "No, it isn't fair. Why now? Why us? How much more do we have to give?" She gripped him tightly.

He gently eased her hands open, then stroked her hair. "You know, every time I went out to fight, I thought it might be for the last time, and that I'd never see you again. I'd never get a chance to say sorry and make things right between us. But we've had this night at least, and maybe we'll have many more. There's plenty of people who haven't been as lucky as us."

Jas's earlier happiness had melted away, but fatigue, or maybe hopelessness, sapped her will to fight him. It seemed to be an inevitability that he would fight in the morning. If that was so, she also had something to get off her chest.

"Carl, I wanted to tell you something too. Something that's important to me for you to know." She told him what had happened to her when she was at training college in Antarctica, and how her experience had made her hold him at arm's length years even though she cared about him. She explained that it was because she cared so much, not because she didn't care enough.

"I'm sorry you went through that," Carl said, "but it explains a lot. I wondered why you acted so weird when we were in Antarctica rescuing Sayen."

"Yeah, I can't stand going back there. Hey, did you know Sayen's aboard?" Jas asked. "She's our navigator. And you remember Toirien MacAdam from the *Galathea*? She's here too."

"Really? No, I didn't know. The minute that I arrived aboard ship I came straight to your cabin. Got some weird looks when I asked where you were. I hope I get time to say hi to both of them before the fight starts tomorrow."

Jas heaved a sigh when he reminded her of the trial ahead. Everything that was about to happen had regained meaning for her. Before, she'd only wanted it all to be over. Now, she was desperate for the Unity Alliance to win and for Carl to survive. But he'd been flying fighters for five years. It was hardly credible that he'd lived this long. Could he survive one more battle?

"I didn't know what had happened to any of you for so long," Carl said. "Then I heard about a new destroyer called the *Thylacine*, and its commander, Jas Harrington, who'd climbed the ranks on merit. They said she was one of the best to serve under." He gave a small smirk.

Jas rolled her eyes and batted him. "The ship's named after you, you know."

"Huh?" Carl lifted himself onto one elbow.

"It's a long story, but one of the admirals has a soft spot for me. When the new ship was commissioned and I was chosen to command it, he asked me for suggestions for a name. They went with the one I picked."

"You think I'm like a rare, predatory marsupial?" Carl asked, one eyebrow raised.

"The Tasmanian tiger came back from extinction, right? When everyone had given up hope."

He sighed, wrapped his arms around her, and buried his face in her neck.

After a little while, Jas said, "Speaking of animals, where's Flux? Is he hiding in your cabin?"

Carl sighed again. "He's gone. He left about four years ago. A planet we freed from the Shadows was his homeland, and he said that now a couple of hundred Earth years had passed, the heat would have died down enough for it to be safe for him to go back."

"He'd been in trouble for something?"

"Yeah. He'd been hiding out. On the run, he said, though he wouldn't tell me what for. Looked sheepish when he talked about it."

Jas wondered how Carl had been able to read the expression on the creature's face. "I'm sorry. You must miss him."

"It was for the best. I didn't want to get the little fella killed. He said to come and visit when it was all over."

When it's all over. Jas hoped with all her heart that it would all be over after tomorrow.

"This admiral who liked you," Carl said. "Was it Pacheco?"

"Yeah, it was. How did you know?"

"Most of the others have three heads, or six legs, or slither rather than walk."

Jas chuckled. He was exaggerating, but he had a point. "We got to know each other when we served together on the *Infineon*. He was in command. It was my first posting."

"So...did you guys get together? It's okay if you did. I don't mind. Five years is a long time." Though he was trying his best to hide it, Jas detected a tone that indicated he *did* mind.

"Nothing happened between me and Pacheco," she replied. She didn't mention the admiral's annoying pursuit of her. "How about you? Did you find someone to keep you company between missions?" Now it was her turn to pretend to not mind.

"I couldn't, Jas. Couldn't stop thinking of you." His eyes showed his raw honesty.

Should she tell him she'd been convinced he was dead? It didn't seem a good idea. That was a conversation for another time.

"I love you," she whispered.

"I love you too."

They both slept.

22

———

Jas's alarm woke her two hours before the *Thylacine* was due to jump to the battle zone. Her stomach sank at the thought that, this time, Carl would be among her fighter pilots. The sound of her alarm hadn't disturbed him, and she studied his tired features with concern. He needed a week of sleep before he would be in a state fit to fly, but she knew he wouldn't allow her to exempt him from duty.

The fact that *she* was the person who might be sending him out to risk his life again seemed unbearably cruel. Just when she thought the Shadow War couldn't ask any more of her, it made another request.

She eased herself out of Carl's arms and went quietly to take a shower. She would delay waking him until it was absolutely necessary. She would leave just enough time for him to eat and dress before the battle hour.

Running her fingers through her hair as she came out of the shower, she was happy to see he was still asleep. But as she was dressing, he woke.

"Good morning, Commander," he said from the bunk as she was buttoning her uniform jacket.

She clicked her tongue. "Don't be an idiot, Carl."

"You look sneck, Jas. And sexy." He got out of the bunk and came over to her. He held her upper arms and leaned forward to kiss her, but stopped.

"Krat," he said, concern overtaking his amorous look. "You're trembling. What's wrong?"

She wrapped her arms around him and pressed her face into his shoulder. "I guess I'm scared."

"Scared?" He rubbed her back. "Jas, you're the bravest person I know."

"No, I don't think I was ever that brave. I just never had much to lose. Not until now."

They stood silently in each other's arms for a while. Jas lifted her head and kissed Carl on the lips. When he kissed her back, though her heart was sad, her body responded. Her breathing quickened and she lifted a hand to unbutton her jacket at her neck. She pulled Carl closer with the other. He helped her with her buttons, and soon they were back in her bunk.

Their lovemaking was more tender and gentle this time. She forgot about anything else. She even forgot where they were and that time was passing—until the loud ringing of her door chime drew her quickly and painfully back to reality.

"Krat," she exclaimed, extricating herself from Carl's embrace and checking the time. "I'm supposed to be speaking to the pilots right now."

"Who's at the door?" Carl asked, picking up his flight suit from where he'd dropped it the night before.

She gave him a worried look. She hoped it wasn't who she thought it was. She hoped it was Trimborn, or Sayen, or anyone else but that person. As she picked up her jacket, she noticed the comm button flashing. How many times had she been called without answering?

She hastily fastened her uniform, then opened the interface screen next to the door. Her stomach fell. It was the last person she wanted to see in the circumstances. Pacheco was right outside, his uniform perfect, and not a hair out of place. He looked annoyed. She winced.

"Carl," she said, "I have to go."

He was pulling his flight suit over his shoulders. He nodded. "Me too."

Jas took a breath and opened her door. She rushed out, knocking Pacheco's shoulder and spinning him around.

"I'm sorry. I'm on my way to the launch bay."

As she ran, she glanced over her shoulder. Pacheco had managed to catch the door before it closed and was looking into her room. Carl appeared, zipping up his flight suit.

Jas cringed and ran on, wishing she'd had time for a better parting from Carl.

23

Carl tried to step around the admiral who was waiting outside Jas's room, but the man blocked his path. He peered at the breast of Carl's flight suit and said, "Pilot Lingiari, I don't think we've met."

Carl finished pulling up his zipper. He guessed this was the admiral who had the hots for Jas. He didn't like the look in the man's eye. It was the look of someone about to throw the first punch, and Carl didn't have time for scrapping with love rivals. He had a ship to fly.

"No," he replied, "I don't think we have." Saluting and asking permission for this or that didn't seem appropriate in the circumstances. "Excuse me." Carl tried to sidestep the admiral again, but the man put a hand on his chest. Carl looked down at the hand and up into the admiral's eyes.

"Being in the commander's cabin first thing in the morning is unprofessional behavior," the admiral said, not blinking. "You're aware that fraternizing while on duty is a court martial offense for both of you?"

Carl tilted his head and looked at the admiral from

under his brows. "What I'm doing in the commander's cabin is none of your business, mate."

The two men locked gazes for a long moment. Anger and pain flitted across the admiral's features, but they were followed by something like resignation. His hand dropped to his side, and Carl took the opportunity to leave. He walked briskly away. He should have been in the launch bay with the rest of the pilots ten minutes ago.

After he had gone twenty or so paces, the admiral called out, "Lingiari."

He stopped and turned.

"You're a lucky man," the admiral said.

Carl paused before replying, "I know."

He jogged through the ship to the launch bay, where the rest of the pilots had already assembled. He snuck behind the fighter ships and slipped in at the back of the group of men and women. Jas had begun speaking to them already. She was talking about how hard and dangerous their job was and that everyone aboard the ship appreciated their service.

She hadn't changed much in the five years since he'd last seen her. She didn't keep herself as fit as she used to, and the strain of command showed on her face. But he found out the previous night and that morning that she was still the same Jas he'd fallen in love with.

She'd said she was scared. He was scared too. Not of the forthcoming battle. He'd lost count of the number he'd flown in the Shadow War. He would try to fly his best as he'd always done. He couldn't do more than that, and that attitude had stood him in good stead until then.

But he knew what Jas had meant when she'd said she was scared of what she had to lose. Now they were together again, he felt the same way. He would have given a lot to jump the *Thylacine* to Earth, fly Jas down to his parents' old farm, and live out the rest of their years quietly. Maybe have a kid or two if Jas was willing. He could teach them to fly.

There had been a time when he'd only dreamed of piloting starships across the galaxy, looking sneck in his pilot's uniform, and flirting with his female shipmates, who he'd imagined would all fall at his feet, of course. That time seemed long ago, and he felt like a different person now. Whether it was living through the Shadow War that had caused his change of heart, or because he'd fallen in love, he didn't know. It didn't matter. He only had to get through today, and maybe his new dreams would come true.

Jas was finishing up her speech. Her gaze had passed over him all the time that she'd been talking, but as she wished them good luck, her eyes met his. For a brief moment, she had the same expression she'd had in her cabin when he'd felt her trembling. The neutral look of command fell away, and her vulnerability and fear showed through.

He wished they'd had time for a proper goodbye. Or maybe it was best that they hadn't.

She turned and left the launch bay. The squadron leader ordered them into their cockpits, ready to respond instantly to the order to join the battle. Carl climbed aboard his fighter and strapped himself in.

It wasn't much of a consolation, but he'd always loved the Unity fighter ship's design. A high cockpit protruding to the front, giving excellent visibility if his scanning equipment failed, and streamlined body with two aerodynamic engines for flying in an atmosphere as well as space. Six low-energy laser emitters faced forward, two on each wing and one on either side of the cockpit. Carl knew these planes' capabilities like the back of his hand.

Just one more flight. Or maybe it wouldn't even come to that.

He yawned and put on his helmet, but opened the visor, which turned off the air and power. Reserving those for when he absolutely needed them had saved his life a couple of times. There weren't many more lonely and isolated experiences than floating in a disabled fighter ship in deep space, waiting for and hoping that someone would be back to pick you up before your oxygen or heat ran out.

The squadron leader's head appeared at Carl's window. "Lingiari?" came the man's voice through his comm. Carl nodded. The man made the universal *open up* gesture. Carl gave the voice command to unlock the hatch, and with the clunk of heavy metal, the ship complied.

"What's up, sir?"

"Step out, pilot. Gotta scan you."

Carl unfastened his safety harness and swung out of the cockpit. The squadron leader ran a Shadow scanner up and down his body. He read the display and nodded. "Just a precaution after your late arrival last night. Can't be too careful. It seems a bit odd to me that we're getting special attention. The *Thylacine's* the only ship with the full complement of pilots. It's like we've been singled out for something."

Carl shrugged, but the man was right. It was a little strange that the authorities had gone to the trouble of reassigning himself and two other pilots to the *Thylacine* at the last minute. The ship was an ordinary destroyer. There was no reason it should be shown any special favor. Jas hadn't said anything about the battle plan.

"Anyway," the squadron leader continued, "glad to have you aboard, Lingiari. I read the service record that arrived with you. I was impressed. It looks like the Unity have sent us their best. You've been in this war longer than I have. Not many have survived so long."

"I've been lucky, sir."

"Takes more than luck to survive the number of fire-fights that you've seen. You could probably teach *me* some maneuvers, but there's no time for that now. You were never promoted to squadron leader?"

"I was offered, but I prefer just to fly."

"Probably wise. Let's get through today, then I'd be glad to share a beer with you later when we celebrate winning this kratting war."

Though the man's words were light, his eyes told of the pilots he'd spoken to in the same manner for the last time.

"I'd be happy to," Carl replied.

The squadron leader ordered him to return to his ship. As Carl refastened his harness, he mulled over the man's suspicions about the role the *Thylacine* was to play in the battle. But after a while he gave up trying to figure out what it might be.

Whatever Jas's task was, it didn't make any difference to him. He would have to do the same job as always: get close enough to the Shadow ship to penetrate its force field with low energy fire, and destroy whatever he was told to destroy. Then get out of there fast before he was caught in the blast if the ship exploded.

For the time being, however, all he had to do was wait. He settled down to mentally replay his recent moments with Jas.

24

J as encountered Sayen as she went from the launch bay to the bridge. In a quarter of an hour, the order would come to jump to the star system where the massive Shadow ship had been spotted. Jas was in a rush, but at the sight of her friend, she had to stop to tell her the news.

As passing crew members moved out of earshot, she said, "Sayen, Carl's here."

"Carl's aboard the ship?" Sayen exclaimed. "He's alive? That's great. When did you see him?"

"Last night. He came to my cabin."

"Oh," Sayen said, smiling. "That must have been quite a reunion. I'm happy for you."

"I'd be happy too, if it weren't for what we have to do today."

"Oh, yeah." Sayen's smile fell. "He's flying, then?"

"I couldn't persuade him not to. I probably could have thought up a reason to excuse him from duty, but he wasn't having it."

Her eyes softening, Sayen said, "If he's made it this far, he can make it through one more battle. I'm sure of it."

"I hope so. I don't know what I'll do if he doesn't. I'd given up on him. I'd given up on everything. Then he came back. If he doesn't survive this, I don't think I'll have a reason to go on."

"Carl will be okay, Jas," Sayen said. "He's a brilliant pilot."

But nothing her friend said could dispel the fear that hung over Jas's heart, and there was no time to talk more with her.

"We'd better go to the bridge," Jas said.

Pacheco was already there. He was standing—there was nowhere for him to sit. As well as overseeing the battle maneuvers of the *Thylacine*, he would help to orchestrate other ships involved in the engagement.

His expression was pained and tight as Jas and Sayen entered the bridge. He didn't look at Jas as she took her seat. Sayen went to her console. The rest of the officers were already at their stations.

"Navigator," Pacheco said, "Please plot our jump."

"Yes, sir." Sayen swiped her screen to activate it and read the display. "Oh," she said. "K.67092d?"

"Yes," Pacheco said between his teeth. "Is there something remarkable about that, Navigator?"

"No, sir," Sayen replied. "I mean, it's only that I've been there before. It's the planet where the commander and I first encountered the Shadows."

The Shadow trap planet. Of course. Jas thought. The planet's designation had been familiar, but she hadn't realized why until Sayen pointed it out. After all these years, they were returning to where it had all begun.

"Hmpf. Yes, it is a Shadow planet," Pacheco said. "One of the earliest ones from what we can gather. Possibly the Shadows have their reasons for parking their mother ship there, but that doesn't concern us today. We'll be fighting this battle in space."

Jas recalled the harsh, windswept, barren surface of K.67092d and the hexagonal structures that the poor fool, Master Loba, had insisted were not constructed by sentient beings. No one had ever discovered how the Shadows made their traps, but there was no doubt about what happened inside them. Myth-addicted, resource-hungry Loba had paid for his thoughtless greed with his life.

Jas gave a shudder. Of all the planets she'd visited while working aboard prospectors, K.67092d was the last place she wanted to return to. She'd rather go back to Antarctica.

"Coordinates ready," Sayen said. "Sending them over."

Pilot Kennewell gave a nod as they arrived. "Jumping in ten."

Jas relayed the information to the crew around the ship, telling them to take their seats. "Perhaps you should find a jumpseat, Admiral?" she asked. It wouldn't be safe for him to be standing when they jumped. Though the process usually wasn't violent, it wasn't unknown for ships to jump into weapons fire.

Pacheco seemed to wrestle with something in his mind, but he conceded to Jas's common sense and left the bridge.

The tension relaxed a little as he departed. Officers who had been intent on their screens looked up and around at each other. There were some nervous smiles and quiet good luck wishes.

Jas tried to clear her mind, and get ready for the battle, but in truth her thoughts were in turmoil. Depending on how the battle went, she faced a terrible decision. If it made tactical sense to scramble the fighters, she would have to do it. And that would mean putting the life of the man she loved at risk.

25

As soon as the *Thylacine* had made the jump, Pacheco began to make his way back to the bridge. The comm officer had set him up with channels to the ships under his command, though his ability to speak with them depended on how effective the Shadow ship's dampening field was.

In the battle where they'd lost the *Camaradon*, it had been all but impossible to comm the other UA ships through space rather than jump channels, but he had to try. The right maneuver at the right time might mean the difference between victory and defeat. In case he couldn't comm the other ships, all their captains and commanders had been fully briefed on the aims and rationale of the battle tactics in case they were forced to act without instruction.

The battle plan was simple: deluge the Shadow ship with fire to prevent it from jumping, surround it with UA ships to dilute the effect of its ray, and give the *Thylacine* time to create the anti-matter bomb. The *Thylacine* would also need their protection while it prepared the bomb.

Jas had to make sure her ship didn't stand out from the

rest. If the Shadows suspected she posed a special threat, all they had to do was target it for destruction with their beam, and the last hope of galactic civilization would be crushed.

That was why the Unity Alliance had chosen the *Thylacine*. There were bigger, faster ships with more firepower, but they would attract the Shadows' attention. The *Thylacine* was a run-of-the-mill destroyer. It wouldn't stand out. It was like a drab brown scorpion with a lethal sting in its tail.

The *Thylacine* was also Jas's ship, and though Pacheco was finally beginning to accept that there would never be anything personal between them, he was still moved to protect her. He'd argued strongly that the *Thylacine* was the right ship for the job.

In a way, he felt a fool. It didn't take a genius to guess that the pilot he'd seen coming out of Jas's cabin that morning was the lost love she'd been pining for all these years. He'd been crushed, if he was honest with himself, to see the man in the flesh. It was one thing to understand on an intellectual level that your love would never be reciprocated; it was quite another to meet your rival face to face.

There wasn't anything special about that man, Lingiari, Pacheco told himself. It was just that he'd made his move first, and Jas wasn't capricious. He knew that. It was one of the things he liked about her.

He was at the bridge. The doors opened and he went in. The battle was already in full swing. The holo of the gigantic Shadow ship hung in the air to the front and center of the bridge. The UA ships ranged around it to the sides and above and below. Farther below, the gray-brown surface of K.67092d with its wide, pale blue oceans slowly turned.

Every ship was firing. Pulses were raining down, but the Shadow ship wasn't using its beam. It must require a period of time to start it up, Pacheco realized. They really had caught the Shadows by surprise this time, unlike at the previous battle where the beam was activated almost immediately.

The Unity Alliance ships were pouring all their energy into attacking the Shadow ship's force field. Pacheco hoped the effort was making a dent in the ship's massive power supply and preventing it from jumping.

He glanced around him as he went over to the comm officer's desk. Everyone on the bridge was performing their tasks like clockwork. Jas sat at the center of the activity, pale and tense. He wondered what was going through her mind. To be reunited with her lover the night before she might lose him in battle had to be tough.

A collective gasp and a flare that lit up the bridge told him before he turned to the holo that the Shadow ship had activated its beam. There it was. The impossibly powerful ray of energy had sprung out and was targeting a UA ship. The Shadows had picked a large battleship out of the numerous UA ships that surrounded it.

The beam bore down, slowly gnawing away at its force field, grinding down its defenses. The battleship ceased firing pulses, as had been the order if targeted by the beam. With luck, the ship would have time to build the energy to jump before the beam broke through.

Meanwhile, the rest of the Unity Alliance fleet targeted their pulses to avoid the ray on their way to the Shadows' force field. If their guess that the beam absorbed the energy from pulses that crossed it was correct, it made no sense to feed it.

The officers were glancing up from their consoles at the battleship that the Shadows had targeted. Jas was also staring at it, her knuckles white as she gripped her armrests.

Suddenly, where the destroyer had been was nothing but empty space. A cheer arose, and Trimborn exclaimed, "They made it. They jumped."

The ray shone out into deep space, fading away at its farthest end. It quickly switched to another ship. This also immediately stopped firing, conserving its energy for its force field and to build up to jump. This ship was smaller, however, and Pacheco doubted it had the ability to withstand the Shadows' beam to the same extent the battleship had.

As if to attract the Shadows' attention, another battleship moved toward the targeted UA ship, but the Shadows didn't take the bait. They poured energy onto the second ship. The battleship inched forward across the holo display, though in reality it was traveling at thousands of kilometers per hour on its RaptorX engines.

Jas murmured into her comm, no doubt checking her engineer's progress with the equipment that was building the anti-matter bomb. Pacheco hoped the bomb was on schedule.

The officers drew in their breath. The Shadows' beam had broken through the second ship's force field, but in another moment it was gone. It was impossible to tell what damage had been done before it jumped. The second ship's crew would soon find out at the other end.

Meanwhile, the battleship that had been trying to distract the Shadows from the weaker ship got her wish. The Shadow's ray flicked to her.

Pacheco had an idea. He asked the comm officer if he had a channel to the other admirals. If they all acted as the battleship had, ordering their ships to fly to the vessel targeted by the ray, they might persuade the Shadows to split their attention. Ten UA ships would withstand a split ray better than one would its concentrated force.

"Sorry, sir," the officer said, "nothing yet, but I'll keep trying."

If they couldn't spread the devastating beam around, the Unity Alliance was playing a losing game. By firing all pulses, the UA ships were expending energy quickly. Few would now be able to do what the first battleship had done and simply jump out of trouble.

They had to last long enough for the *Thylacine* to launch the anti-matter bomb.

Even without Pacheco's suggestion, many of the UA ships seemed to have had the same idea. They flew toward the battleship that was under fire. But the Shadows were not to be tempted. From experience, Pacheco knew the battleship's force field could not last much longer. He caught Jas's worried gaze as they both counted down the seconds.

The beam broke through the battleship's force field. A minute later, her hull began to break down. Soon, she was gone.

"Did they have time to evacuate?" someone asked.

"Concentrate on your job," Jas snapped.

Another ship blinked into existence to the far side of the Shadow ship. It was the first battleship, returning to the fight. The Shadow ship saw her immediately, and left its target to fire again upon the returned ship.

The pulses the UA vessels were pouring at the Shadow ship's force field seemed to make no difference to its resources. The beam didn't lessen, dim, or waver. The ship's power levels were incredible.

Another ship appeared and began firing on the returned battleship. Pacheco's momentary confusion cleared. It was another Shadow ship. The mother ship was calling her children to her. Another Shadow ship appeared, and another. The battle became difficult to follow as the new Shadow ships engaged with UA vessels, forcing them to re-target their pulses.

The returned battleship lost her fight. She burst apart.

How much longer for the anti-matter bomb? Time was dragging. They'd been fighting less than half an hour, yet it seemed much longer. Had something gone wrong with the bomb? Pacheco couldn't ask Jas directly. None of the officers present knew of the UA's plan. The danger that something would be leaked to the Shadows had been too great.

"They're sending out fighters," exclaimed Trimborn.

From the underside of the giant Shadow ship, a cloud of sparks streamed like hornets from a nest. The Shadow mother ship was going all out to attack the UA vessels. Pacheco swung to Jas with a sudden realization. If any approached the *Thylacine*, she would be forced to respond. Not to do so would be odd, and she couldn't afford to do anything to attract the Shadows' attention. The *Thylacine* wouldn't last long under that dreadful beam.

Another UA ship exploded, and the ray sought a new victim. More Shadow ships appeared. The tide of the battle was turning against the Unity Alliance. They had to deploy the anti-matter bomb, and soon. The chances that the *Thylacine* would be next to experience the Shadows' beam grew stronger every moment.

"Fighters approaching, ma'am," Trimborn said, though his words were unnecessary. The contingent of Shadow fighters approaching the *Thylacine* was plain to see.

"Target pulses on them," Jas said.

The *Thylacine's* pulses diverted from the Shadow mother ship and onto the approaching fighter ships. The small specks were undeterred by the bolts that passed through them, hitting only one or two. The *Thylacine* had to use a different method to defend herself from their attack.

Jas's face was wracked with pain as she spoke into her comm, and Pacheco lip-read the words, "Squadron Leader, scramble fighters."

26

Jas could barely concentrate on the battle. Her thoughts and heart were with Carl, who was at that moment flying out of the safety of the *Thylacine* to do battle with Shadow fighters once more. In her mind's eye, she could see him intent over the controls of his ship, guiding it skillfully into space, seeking out the approaching Shadow ships, ready to fire.

Like all the other pilots, he was also tasked with breaking through the Shadow fighters' ranks and attacking the origin point of the Shadows' devastating weapon in the hope of disabling or destroying it, slim though the chances were of their success.

And Carl wouldn't shirk his duty, Jas knew, even though he'd done far more than his fair share of fighting.

Her gaze was fixed on the swirling sparks that were the *Thylacine's* fighters, already drawing near the enemy. The rest of the battle faded in significance compared to those tiny flecks of life. The two sets of fighters engaged, and the sparks began to disappear.

"MacAdam," she said urgently into her comm. "How long?"

"Thirty-seven seconds, ma'am," came the reply.

The anti-matter bomb had been configured to be attracted to the greatest source of energy in the immediate area. It needed no aiming to fly directly to the Shadow's beam. Once released, it would do its job. The question was only whether it would succeed. The idea that the beam absorbed as well as dispensed energy was just a hypothesis. The Transgalactic Council scientists were also unsure that they had effectively disguised the bomb as a pulse, or that it wouldn't explode before it reached its destination.

It was all based on guesswork. If they were wrong, it was all over.

Jas realized she was biting the edge of her thumb and the iron taste of blood was in her mouth. She couldn't take her eyes off the part of the holo where the *Thylacine* and Shadow fighters were at battle.

"Toirien," she exclaimed into her comm.

"It's ready," Toirien said.

"Fire now," Jas blurted.

A pulse flew out from the *Thylacine* toward the Shadow ship. It looked the same as the others, and Jas could only tell it was the bomb because it didn't follow the same trajectory. Rather than targeting the side of the ship opposite the beam, it flew straight toward it.

"Hey," Trimborn said, "what's that? Is it one of ours?"

"Pilot, reverse Raptors," Jas barked. If the bomb worked, there was going to be one hell of an explosion.

Looking confused but obeying immediately, Kennewell pulled the ship sharply away. Pacheco stumbled due to the sudden movement.

With some relief, Jas saw that the fighter pilots had

noticed the *Thylacine's* motion and broken off their engagement to return to her. She didn't worry about leaving them behind, despite her speed. Until the *Thylacine* built momentum, the fighters could fly much faster and catch up to her easily.

The other UA ships were also quickly withdrawing from the vicinity of the Shadow ship. Their captains and commanders had clearly been watching for the release of the anti-matter bomb, as their ships began to crawl steadily away.

The bomb reached the Shadows' beam and was gone in a flash. Jas and Pacheco were the only ones on the bridge who understood the significance of the event. Jas stared at the beam, though the brilliant light hurt her eyes. One second passed, and another. The bomb should have reached the ship. It should have exploded.

Nausea rose in her stomach. The bomb hadn't worked. They'd failed. She locked gazes with Pacheco. His dark eyes were full of despair.

Then the Shadow mother ship exploded. The *Thylacine* was thrown backward at ten times her earlier speed. The holo disappeared as the ship's sensors were flooded. Jas gripped her armrests to avoid being thrown out of her seat. Pacheco was already down.

"Hull breached," Trimborn said in a strangled tone, holding tight to his console.

But there wasn't anything anyone could do until the force of the Shadow ship's explosion had dissipated. They waited for the turbulent movement to ease. Gradually, the forces operating on the *Thylacine* diminished. Jas's hold on her armrests loosened, and Pacheco stood up.

"Damage report," she said.

"Where do I start?" Trimborn asked.

She snapped a hard look at him, and he said hastily, "Hull breached decks five through eight. Two RaptorX's out. I don't know about the jump engines. Not getting anything from them."

"How about the sensors?" Jas asked. "Can we get the holo back up?"

She desperately wanted to see what had happened to the fighter ships in that devastating blast.

"External sensors are knocked out," Trimborn said. "They're auto-repairing, but give no estimate on completion time. Internal sensors are operational."

Krat. There was only one way she could tell if Carl had survived. When he returned to the ship, the internal sensors would pick up the signal from his chip.

She stood up. "I'll be in my office," she announced.

"Commander," Pacheco said, "aren't you forgetting something?"

"What?" Jas answered, before realizing her officers were watching and waiting for an explanation of what had just happened. "Oh, yes. We just destroyed the Shadow mother ship."

The women and men around her gaped. They looked to Pacheco for confirmation that their commander hadn't gone mad. When he nodded his agreement, they began to whoop and holler and hug each other.

Jas left the bridge unnoticed as her officers celebrated. She went quickly to her office. Someone on the bridge broadcast the news of the victory around the ship, and the celebrations spread.

Until Jas knew Carl was aboard the ship, she couldn't join in.

At her office, she sat and turned on her interface. The list of pilots was already on the screen. The names refreshed as the computer added the data on the pilots who had arrived the previous night. There was Carl's name. No light was beside it.

It's okay, she told herself. *It's still early.* She couldn't expect to see any of the returning pilots yet. The Shadow ship's explosion must have propelled them all over the place. It might take them hours to make their way back to the *Thylacine.* And some of the ships would be disabled. They would have to sweep for them. Other ships might pick them up.

Jas reassured herself in this way over the next few hours as buttons lit up next to the returning pilots' names. Sayen came to see her and watch with her, but Jas sent her away. She didn't want any distraction from the screen. Pacheco also came in, to see what she was doing. As soon as he realized, he told her he would take over the running of the ship while she was busy. She barely heard him.

Carl didn't arrive with the pilots who managed to return to the *Thylacine* under their own power.

They didn't find him in any of their sweeps. None of the other UA ships had picked him up.

Twenty-four hours later, after a night of no sleep, Jas finally accepted he was gone.

The Shadow War was over, and it didn't mean a thing.

27

In the days that followed the Unity Alliance's victory in the Shadow War, Sayen had little to do. She spent most of her time worrying about Jas. The *Thylacine* remained at the scene of the battle, in orbit around K.67092d. The ship's defense units and troops were planet-side destroying the Shadow traps. There were many, so the task was a long and difficult one.

The rebuilding of galactic civilization had yet to begin, but the mopping up process after the war was underway. The Unity Alliance ships set out to find and destroy the remaining Shadow ships and free the planets in the sector that remained under their control. The UA had to be sure the galaxy was free of the Shadow menace. After that, all sentient species would have to remain in constant vigilance to prevent them from returning from the Void and establishing strongholds again.

Jas remained in her quarters most of the time, dele-gating whatever tasks she could, refusing to talk to anyone. The first couple of times Sayen had visited, Jas had been polite, saying she was too busy or tired to talk. The third time she'd been more abrupt.

Sayen had been standing outside Jas's cabin, speaking into her comm—her friend wouldn't even open the door. "Jas, please let me in. I just want to talk. It helps, you know. It might not seem like it, but it does."

"I can't see you now," came Jas's reply, "as I've already said. Stop bothering me, Navigator. That's an order."

There was something in her friend's tone that didn't sound quite right. It wasn't that she sounded unhappy—that was to be expected. It was something else.

"Don't be like that," Sayen said. "I thought we were friends. Why are you talking to me about orders?"

"Because I'm your kratting commander. Now do as you're told."

Sayen could hardly believe what she was hearing.

"Jas, open the door. I'm really worried about you. If you don't open up, I'll tell the doctor you're sick and he'll override your door security."

There was no reply, but thirty seconds later, the door opened. Jas stood on the other side, fury written on her features. "What will it take to get you to leave me alone?" she spat.

Sayen reeled back, and not only from her friend's venom. She reeked of alcohol.

"You're drunk," Sayen exclaimed.

"What I do in my private time is none of your business," Jas said. "Now, *will* you go away?"

"No," Sayen replied. "No, I'm not going anywhere. You need help. You can't deal with this by yourself."

"Oh right. What kind of *help* do you think you're going to get me? What do *you* think is going to make me feel better?"

"Jas, don't forget that I've been through this. I know how

you feel."

"You...you know how I feel? Is that some kind of joke? You think this is like you and Erielle?" She swallowed. "He's dead, Sayen. Carl's gone, and it's *my* fault. I sent him out there to die. So unless you killed the person you loved, you have *no* idea how I feel, and you have no idea what's going to put things right. Nothing can bring him back and *nothing* can change what I did."

"What? You didn't send him to—"

The door slid closed. Sayen called Jas through the comm a few more times, but her friend wouldn't answer.

She wasn't sure what to do. If Jas wouldn't talk to her, she didn't know who she would talk to. She didn't want to tell the admiral what was going on—he would probably relieve Jas of her duties and her duties might be the only thing keeping her going.

In search of advice and someone to share her worries with, she went to see the only other person aboard who really knew Jas. Maybe together they could figure out how to help her.

Toirien MacAdam was working in the jump engines, running point by point diagnostics, the second engineer said. Sayen went to an engine access hatch and climbed down the narrow ladder. As she went, she was strongly reminded of the time that she, Jas, and Carl had hidden from Shadows in the engine of the *Galathea*. It seemed like another lifetime.

Her vision blurred, and she blinked to clear it as she remembered Carl. She hadn't even had a chance to see him when he came aboard the *Thylacine*. Though it had been five years since they'd parted at Ganymede Station, her affection toward him hadn't lessened. He'd been like a brother to her. Jas wasn't the only one grieving over his loss.

Within the access tunnels to the huge jump engines, the ship's noises were cut off. Sayen heard Toirien's footsteps in the quietness as she walked the steel mesh floor. By following their sound and calling her name, Sayen soon found the engineer.

Toirien listened carefully to Sayen as she explained the situation. She turned to the control panel she was working at and pressed some keys before answering.

"Well, it's certainly strange how things turn around," she said.

"Huh?"

"The last time Jas Harrington and I were working aboard the same ship, it was me who was getting drunk, and worse."

"Seriously?" Sayen said. Toirien had told her of her former addictions, but she hadn't said she'd continued them aboard ship. "Did Jas or Carl know?"

"Oh yeah. Jas knew. She found me off my legs in my bunk one time. Outraged, she was, and rightly so. Everyone was relying on me to get the *Galathea's* engines working again. The only problem was, I knew it. I couldn't take the pressure. And I missed my girls. I...well, it's a long story. It just strikes me as an odd coincidence that mine and Jas's circumstances are the other way around now."

"So...what changed?" Sayen asked. "What helped you give it up?"

"Ha." Toirien smiled wryly. "I don't think what helped me is going to be of any use to poor Jas." She returned her attention to the control panel.

After Sayen had waited expectantly for a moment or so, Toirien relented and said, her face reddening, "It was a myth run."

Sayen's eyes widened. "You were a myth addict?"

"Not exactly. That takes serious creds. But old Loba was,

and after he died, his stash was found and distributed around the ship. I got a hold of a dose. I was as low as I could go. And…" Her face went redder still. "You know, now that I come to think of it, I've never told anyone this.

"I went on my myth run, and I had a strange dream. I was floating in bliss, when some beautiful creatures came to me. They took me to my daughters, who were much younger in my dream than they were at the time. They were the same ages they had been when I'd last seen them. I was so happy to be with them again. Then, the strangest part of the dream was that my eldest told me I was being stupid. She said there was nothing wrong with the engines, and that it was only my doubting myself that was holding me back."

Sayen's eyes grew wider and her jaw dropped. "And was it true?"

"It was true. I hadn't trusted myself to interpret the readings I was getting from the engines. They were fine. I hadn't believed the evidence of my eyes. When we tried them, they worked. Carl got us off the planet, and we were saved."

"I remember," Sayen exclaimed. "Carl told me you thought the engines wouldn't start because we were on emergency power after the crash. But as far as I can remember, Jas only said that you finally figured out the engines were okay."

"I don't think she knew any more than that. It wasn't like I went around advertising what I'd done."

Sayen sighed. "It's an interesting story, but I think you're right. A myth run isn't gonna help Jas. That isn't going to help her forgive herself."

"No. I'm sorry, I don't know what to suggest. Maybe with time she'll start to get over it. It's early days. The wound's still raw."

"Yeah, maybe," Sayen said, but from what she knew of Jas, she wasn't sure that was likely to happen.

She thanked Toirien for her time and climbed out of the access tunnels. She decided she would try one more time to talk to Jas and persuade her to see the doctor. If she refused, Sayen would tell the doctor herself. Jas needed help, whether she realized it or not. She headed toward her friend's quarters once again.

But she found Jas before she reached her destination. Her friend was standing in a passageway with her back to a bulkhead. Now that Sayen could see her under the bright overhead lights, she saw that Jas looked worse than she'd ever seen her. She looked like she hadn't eaten in days. Her facial bones jutted out of her skin and her clothes were loose on her body. Her hair was a mess. Her lips were pale, and her eyes were sunken in their orbits. They had a strange, faraway look.

"Jas?" Sayen said. "Did you change your mind? Are you going to see the doc? Do you want to talk?"

Her friend didn't reply. She was looking at her as though she didn't know who Sayen was. Then her gaze shifted straight ahead of her to the opposite bulkhead.

Except it wasn't a wall. It was an airlock.

Sayen's heart froze. "Jas, hun. What're you fixing to do?" She took a step toward her friend. Jas slid an equal distance away. She was looking longingly at the airlock hatch. Sayen's throat was constricting. Could she stop her friend from going into the airlock if it came to it? She probably could, but she didn't want to take that risk.

Her heart sinking, Sayen lifted her comm button to her lips and, not taking her eyes from Jas, she called Admiral Pacheco.

28

"You can remain in your quarters for the time being," Pacheco said. "Unless you'd rather stay in the sick bay? There would be people around you, and you wouldn't be alone. The doctor could monitor you better."

Jas was on her bunk. Her feet were on the floor and her head was down. She barely heard what the man was saying. She was in civilian clothes, having been relieved of duties for an undefined length of time.

"I really think it would be a good idea for you to stay in the sick bay," Pacheco said.

Why wouldn't he leave her alone? She wished they would all leave her alone. She couldn't be around people. It hurt too much. Everything hurt too much.

"Jas?"

She shook her head. "M'okay." The sedation was making it hard to speak, and she could hardly think. But then again, maybe that was a good thing.

"Right," said Pacheco. "As long as you're sure. You *are* sure you're feeling better?" 'Better' meant that she wasn't going to space herself. Everyone wanted her to be 'better'. Jas didn't want to be better. All she wanted was Carl back, or to never have sent him to his death.

She mustered her concentration. "I'm okay. Really." Anything to make the man go away.

Pacheco moved toward the door. "I'll leave you for a while, then. Navigator Lee will be along to see you soon, in case you need anything." He paused. "Jas, I'm sorry. You waited for your pilot for so long, he must have meant a lot to you. When I saw him coming out of your cabin, I could have put him in the brig. That would have kept him out of the battle. It would have been easy enough. I could have protected him for you, but I didn't. I didn't even think of it. I guess I was just too wrapped up in myself."

At the edge of her vision, Jas saw Pacheco's legs and feet at the door. She wished he would leave. Didn't he understand she had enough of her own *what ifs* to occupy her forever? She didn't need his too.

Finally, he left.

She lay down on her bunk and curled up on her side. After a long time, during which Sayen arrived to check on her, she slept.

When she woke up, she felt terrible. Slivers of pain stabbed behind her eyes, her tongue was thick in her mouth, and her throat ached. She wondered if it was a side-effect of the sedation. She sat up, wincing as the movement caused more pain to dance behind her eyes. Her eyelids squeezed to slits, she checked the time. She'd been asleep around four hours. It was the quiet shift aboard the ship. Most everyone would be asleep.

She pulled up her sleeve to where the sedation dispenser was taped to the underside of her arm, and picked at the edges of the tape until she could peel it off. The dispenser was a lozenge of plastic with a fine mesh opening, through which the sedative was forced into her bloodstream at regular intervals.

Now that the tape was gone, the dispenser was only lightly stuck to her skin. She removed it and put it in the trash. She went to her wash basin and doused her face with water.

Not really knowing what she was going to do, she left her cabin. Though the doctor had infused calories into her system to make up for her days of self-starvation, taking away her dizziness, her legs remained unsteady from the doses of sedation. She rested a hand on the bulkhead as she went along to keep her balance.

She drew closer to an airlock. She thought she knew the code to open it. It was to access a sensor array for external repair.

If she went through the lock, it would mean a quick end to her pain. To die like that, frozen and floating among the stars, seemed kind of fitting. On the other hand, maybe she didn't deserve a quick end. It seemed too easy after what she'd done.

She passed the airlock by, saving the option for another time.

Wandering aimlessly through the quiet passageways, she realized she was making her way to the crew living sections. These were the dirtier, noisier parts of the ship, where the lowest-ranking crew bunked four to a cabin, and quiet and privacy were scarce. It had been a long time since Jas had lived in those conditions, when she'd been a plain security officer. Young and lonely. Had anything much changed? Now she was older and lonely, that was all.

The area wasn't very familiar. She rarely came this way. She'd hated the way all the lowest ranks would leap to attention when she appeared. She'd felt like she was invading the one place they had where they could relax. But now she was no longer a commander. She wasn't anything. She had no doubts she would be retired on health grounds as soon as the sweep of the Shadow trap planet was complete and the *Thylacine* returned to Unity docking.

She came across a door she vaguely remembered was the entrance to a lounge. She was tired, and she wanted to sit down. Thinking the place would probably be empty at that hour, she opened the door. Four pairs of eyes turned to her. Four crew members were huddled together over something on a low table.

For a second, she and the men and women stared at each other, then one of them shouted, "It's the commander." They all bolted, pushing her down in their rush to leave the room. Dazed, she looked behind her, but they were gone.

She rose unsteadily to her feet and went over to the spot where the crew members had been huddled. A small opaque bottle was on the table, along with some drug-taking paraphernalia. She sat down and picked up the bottle, an idea of what might be in it already forming. The bottle was tiny. After unscrewing the lid, she peered inside. She had to put her head close to look through the small hole, and as she did so, a whiff of vapor from the contents confirmed her suspicion. Just a breath of the substance made her head spin.

It was myth.

Someone had smuggled myth aboard. Her attempts to weed out the addicts hadn't been entirely successful. Automatically, she reached for her comm button to inform Pacheco, but it wasn't there. She'd forgotten to transfer it from her uniform. She looked up at the door. Next to it was a comm console that would also allow her to do the right thing and tell someone what she'd found.

But that small barrier to action had given her time to think. She'd only experienced the effects of myth once—on Ganymede Station when the Council managers had wanted a volunteer to try to communicate with the Paths. But since that time she had never lost the hankering to try it again. The visit to the mythrin mine had concentrated the feeling.

Up until that moment, she'd always managed to resist the temptation.

She put the lid back on the bottle and held it in her palm, cool and smooth. It was so small, it probably only held one or at most two doses, yet aboard the ship it would sell for a month's wages. Jas recalled the experience of her myth run. She remembered how all concerns and fears had fallen away, and she had basked in perfect, seemingly endless bliss.

The prospect of escaping from the hell she was in—real escape, not the dulling of every emotion that the sedative gave—was tantalizing. The idea that she could forget that Carl was gone, if only for a few hours, grew stronger in her mind.

She picked up the paraphernalia, slipped it with the bottle of myth into her pocket and left the lounge.

29

As soon as she'd closed her door, Jas took out the bottle of myth and box of needles and swabs from her pocket and quickly stripped off her clothes. She wanted to start the myth run soon or she might be discovered before it was over. She had the feeling she was standing on the precipice of a vast, black abyss, yet she didn't care.

Before lying down in her bunk, she unscrewed the bottle, plunged the needle into the crimson liquid and drew it all up into the syringe. The myth was a deep, dark carmine in the dimmed cabin light, like blood. Her heart raced at the thought of the escape that it held. She'd been right when she told Carl that she wasn't brave. There were some things she couldn't face, and this precious drug was her way out, for a few hours at least.

She lay down, holding up the hypodermic syringe in one hand. Closing her eyes, she brought back the memory of when Sparks had injected the drug into her. The site of the injection was important, she'd heard. She bit her lip. The memory of the bolt of pain that had shot through her when the myth entered her system was still vivid, but it was worth it for what happened after.

She traced the fingers of her other hand down one side of her belly, trying to recall the exact spot. Her action reminded her of her night with Carl, and she whimpered from a hurt more painful than any she'd ever felt in all her years of fighting. She clenched her teeth. Just a few more moments, and the terrible ache would be gone. Her fingers probed farther south until she located the spot where she was certain she'd received her last shot of myth. She opened her eyes and lifted her head from her pillow, gazing down at the area.

She positioned the hypodermic syringe above the spot and hesitated. The tiniest flicker of sense at the back of her mind told her that what she was doing was wrong. But she pushed the thought away as she simultaneously plunged the needle into her skin.

The agony as she pressed the plunger home caused her to cry out, but the sound died on her lips as the drug took effect.

SHE WAS FLOATING FREE, unchained from her pain, and it was bliss. Now that she'd returned here, she remembered the Void as clearly as if she'd never left. Its otherness was impossible to put into the language of the physical plane, but she was aware of infinite distance, light, and color.

She was also infinite and without form. She reached out to the vast ends of the Void, then contracted smaller than an electron. She reveled in the endless space, where nothing and everything had happened and time did not exist. Carl had not died. They were together and apart, and it didn't matter. Nothing mattered anymore. She would stay in the Void forever.

After she had drifted for always and for no time at all, something told her she wasn't alone. Presences were approaching her consciousness. Unease rippled through her as a vague memory of something unpleasant about the Void surfaced. There were some beings here who trapped people—who had trapped her. She recalled fighting and an escape back to the other place.

But her senses told her these were not those beings. Her tension eased. These were the ones who had fought for her. These beings had come through to the physical plane to help her and others. She found it hard to remember where she'd come from. Consciousness of the other side was slippery in her mind. That place felt unreal. Here was reality and truth.

The beings of the Void spoke. "We know you," they said. "You came to us in the other place. You saved us when we were weak and helpless."

"Did I?" Jas's unspoken words echoed inside her. "I don't remember."

"You have been here with us before."

"Yes, and now I've come back, and I'm staying."

"You cannot remain. Your kind can never remain. You always go back."

"I'm not going back." Dark gray ripples of disquiet left her and spread out.

"You will."

She twisted and turned, trying to escape the beings, but they were everywhere that she was, around her and within her. She rejected their message. Why wouldn't they let her mind return to floating free and careless?

"Many of the Others are gone," the beings said,

"destroyed on the physical plane. We are sad that they harmed so many of you, but we are grateful that their existence has been reduced and they no longer trouble us."

The beings' words were sparking painful recollections in her mind. She wished they would stop. "Please, leave me."

"We will depart if our presence disturbs you, but we came to tell you the one you mourn is here."

The words reverberated through her perception. *The one I mourn?*

"...What?"

"The one whose loss you grieve is here, but he cannot exist in the Void. He is fading."

"What?" Jas's unspoken voice was tiny.

"You ache. You have suffered a loss. We can sense this. The one you have lost is here."

Struggling hard against the mind-numbing effects of being in the Void, Jas said without words, "Carl's here?"

"If that is how you identify him using language, that one is here. We can sense him in you, but he is here too."

"Where? Take me to him."

"He is here as you are, but you cannot sense him."

"Can he sense me?"

"No."

Despair nibbled the numbed edges of Jas's consciousness. Even in the Void there was no escape from it. Her escape was no escape after all.

"Should we return him to your universe?" the beings asked. "He may not survive the transition, but he also cannot survive here."

"You can send him back? I don't understand. Haven't the Shadows got him? Won't he come back as a Shadow?"

"We have the remaining Others under control. We can use their mechanism to push him through at the place where you found us. But the Others use their process to insert their persona into the newly created copy of the one they stole. We will eschew this part. We will not insert a persona."

"No persona?" Jas couldn't grasp their meaning. Carl wouldn't be Carl? Just his body? She struggled to comprehend, but her thoughts were slippery and ephemeral. "Can you explain?"

"The Others recreated only the form of the creatures from the physical plane. They animated the copies they made with their own selves. If we return the one you lost, he will have no self."

She still couldn't really understand. It sounded like whatever they pushed through would have Carl's brain with all its knowledge and memories, but somehow he wouldn't have his personality. She couldn't imagine what Carl would be like if the beings did as they proposed. But just to have him back would be something.

"What should we do?" the beings asked.

"Send him back. Please, send him back."

"We will return him to the place where you found us."

SHE OPENED HER EYES. She was lying naked in her bunk, a hypodermic needle hanging painfully from her upper thigh. She sat up and carefully pulled out the needle. The syringe was empty. As she remembered what she'd done and why, the weight of her entire existence settled heavily over her.

So it had all come to this? All her years of fighting. Everything she'd endured. All the friends that she'd dragged into the fight, only to have them die. And she'd ended up like the man she'd despised—Loba, a myth addict, living only for the next run.

The syringe in her hand fell from her fingers to the floor. Let it lie there. Let them see it. What did she care? Her mind returned to the airlock and its alluring escape.

She rose out of her bunk and went into the shower. Maybe she could wash away some of the disgust she felt for herself. As the hot water started up, she was reminded of the shower she took the morning that she saw Carl for the last time.

She groaned. She rested her forearm on the shower wall and her forehead on her arm while the water cascaded over her. She would never be able to clean herself of what she'd done. She'd never be free of her all-pervading grief. Everywhere she went and everything she did reminded her of him.

Sometime later—she didn't know how long—she turned off the water and got out of the shower. Her efforts to divert her mind from thoughts of Carl were useless, and something about him was nagging away at her like a toothache. A background annoyance that she couldn't bring to the front of her mind.

She put on some clothes and sat on her bunk, slumped forward. Checking the time, she was surprised to see only around two or three hours had passed since she'd injected the myth. As she understood it, she should have been out for at least five or six hours. She rubbed the inner corners of her eyes with her fingertips.

Carl. There was something important she had to remember about Carl. Something about... She squeezed her eyes shut and forced her foggy mind to clear. Snippets of her myth run flashed into her inner vision. The benevolent beings—the Paths—had been there, and there was something else, something to do with Carl. The Paths had told her...what was it?

Jas gasped. Her hands gripped her bunk.

The Paths had told her Carl was in the Void and they were going to send him back.

30

———

Jas hammered on Kennewell's door. Then she remembered about door chimes and pressed that too. Before the pilot had time to answer, she pressed again.

"Kennewell," she called through the door, "wake up. I want you to take me planetside. Now. Kennewell!"

Jas didn't let up until the pilot's door opened and the tousled-haired young woman appeared, staring at her with sleepy eyes.

"Commander?" she said, covering a yawn with the back of her hand.

"I need you to take me planetside in the shuttle immediately. I have the coordinates."

"But, I, er...Are you sure that's a good idea?" Kennewell's returning memory that Jas had been relieved of her duties was evident in her expression.

"Yes, I'm sure. But if I told you why, you wouldn't believe me. You'll have to trust me. It's about Carl Lingiari, one of the lost pilots. I think I might have a chance of finding him."

"Oh." Kennewell's face turned sad and sympathetic. It

was clear she thought Jas was so grief-stricken, she was delusional. Her face brightened as something occurred to her. "Okay, ma'am. Sure. I just need to ask the admiral for permission first."

"No, you can't." Jas took a deep breath and tried to calm herself. She had to convince Kennewell to take her down to K.67092d. She'd known the pilot for years. She was almost a friend. "Look, I know how it looks. You think I'm crazy. I was. I was out of my mind with grief. But I'm not now. And I really, really need you to do this for me. Please. As a favor. I was a good commander, wasn't I? I was fair? Not like Pacheco?"

"Actually, you and he are pretty alike."

"What?"

"Never mind." Kennewell sighed. "I'm probably going to regret this, but the war's over and I'm going home soon, so what the hell. Okay. I'll take you down. Just let me get dressed." The door closed.

Jas waited impatiently for Kennewell to emerge, and when she did, she hurried the pilot toward the launch bay.

"You've cleared this, right?" Kennewell asked as they went along. "It's not like I can just take a shuttle and fly it wherever I want."

Krat. "No, I haven't. What do you suggest?"

"Hmm...well, if Trimborn's on duty, we should be okay. He might turn a blind eye and let me go."

"Really? How come?" Jas was surprised to hear that her first officer would act so unprofessionally.

"We, er, we have a thing going on."

"You do? Well, that's great. I hope it's him." Jas also hoped that Pacheco was still asleep. If he found out what she was doing, he'd probably have her restrained. She was well aware that telling him about her myth run and what the Paths had told her would be useless. He would only think she was still insane with grief and guilt. Sayen might believe her, but she didn't have time to convince anyone. The Paths had said that Carl was fading and that they would push him into the physical plane, but she didn't know when.

Troops and defense units were in the process of destroying all the Shadow traps on the planet. If she didn't get there soon, she might be too late.

The guards at the launch bay were nonplussed by Jas turning up in civilian clothes with Kennewell at her side. Jas put on her best serious commander face and nodded at them as she walked swiftly past. The guards fell for her bluff and didn't challenge her.

It had taken Jas some serious digging to find the coordinates of the crash site of the *Galathea*, but she'd located them in the data files on K.67092d. The shuttle had a copilot's seat, which Jas took. As she sat down next to her, Jas gave Kennewell the coordinates.

She let the pilot do the talking when it came to persuading Trimborn to okay the shuttle launch. Kennewell framed the request in terms of the commander's receiving information about a lost pilot that she wanted to informally investigate. Trimborn didn't sound like he believed her, but he allowed them to go.

Jas closed her eyes and tried to relax as Kennewell piloted the shuttle planetside. She doubted that the Paths truly understood time, coming from a place where it didn't exist. Carl could have already come through into the Shadow trap and be wandering around somewhere that was just about to be destroyed.

But there wasn't anything she could do to arrive faster. At her urging, Kennewell was already flying the shuttle at its maximum speed.

"Commander," Kennewell said, "do you really think you can find this pilot? We did a thorough sweep."

Jas opened her eyes. "We couldn't sweep the place where he's been. I think what happened was that after a dogfight or the explosion of the Shadow mother ship, he crash landed on K.67092d. Maybe he crashed right into a trap or got carried into one unconscious. I don't know. There weren't any Shadows on the planet when I was there, but that was a long time ago. However it happened, he was taken into the Void. Except there are so few Shadows there now, the benevolent beings who also live there have stopped them from returning. They're sending Carl back minus a Shadow's personality."

"But how do you know? Who told you?"

"That's a long story. I hope I have the chance to tell it to you one day."

31

L anding at the site of the *Galathea's* crash gave Jas a weird, uncomfortable feeling. In spite of the passage of years, the crash site was plain to see as they came down. A wide, deep trench was carved into the rocky soil, with a yawning hole at the end of it where the starship had slid to a halt and, later, the Shadows had begun to draw it down into their trap.

One thing was very different. A team of troops and defense units were walking away from the trap toward a military vehicle parked about a kilometer away. Jas knew this sight well. The troops were sweeping the planet for traps, and they were about to blow this one up.

Except that she wasn't going to let them.

Before the shuttle had come to a stop, Jas was undoing her harness. She jumped out of her seat.

"Let me turn off the engines, for krat's sake," Kennewell said.

The air was hot with heat exhaust when the pilot finally opened the hatch and allowed Jas to leave the shuttle. Their arrival had had the effect she'd hoped it would. The troops and units had paused and were watching curiously as she ran toward them.

"You can't blow this one up," she shouted as soon as she was within hearing distance. "Someone's inside."

The corporal in charge put his hand on his hips at her words. He was a grizzled old soldier who would have been too far on in years to fight if they hadn't been at war. Jas didn't recognize him. He must have been drafted in for the work from another ship.

The man looked at Jas with narrowed eyes as she reached the group, panting. She was definitely out of shape.

"You mustn't destroy this trap," Jas gasped.

"Says who?" the corporal asked, looking her up and down.

Jas had been hoping to use her former authority to persuade the troops to obey her, but they were all strangers. To them, she was just a Martian in civvies.

"I'm Commander Harrington."

Comprehension dawned in the older man's eyes. "Oh, right." He gave a smirk. He'd obviously heard of her fall from grace. "Sorry, ma'am. We're just obeying orders. Now if you have something from the admiral...?"

Jas clenched her fists. "There's no time for that. If you blow up that trap you'll be killing a man. A pilot. He crashed here." As she spoke the lie, Jas realized how crazy she had to sound. There was clearly no sign of a crashed fighter ship. Carl must have come down somewhere else. It was here that the Paths were returning him.

"Yeah, sure," the corporal said, nodding and winking at his troops, who were barely controlling their smiles. "You should get back to your shuttle, ma'am, or you'll be in the blast zone."

"No," Jas exclaimed. "Listen to me."

But the corporal had signaled his troops and units to follow him. They turned their backs and began to walk away. Jas sized up the group. Five soldiers and three units. She could never take them all. She swung around to look for Kennewell, hoping that maybe the pilot had a weapon on her.

As she turned in the direction of the Shadow trap, she saw him.

Carl was emerging from the hexagonal entrance. His head was down, and he was staggering, but it was him. He was alive.

"Carl," Jas yelled as she sprinted over to him.

Her cry attracted the attention of the troops.

"It's a Shadow," one of them cried.

Jas glanced back, and with horror saw one of them lift his weapon to fire.

"No," she shouted, and put herself between the soldier and Carl. "Don't shoot. He isn't a Shadow."

"Out of the way, ma'am," the corporal yelled. "Get out of the way."

But Jas continued to run. The closer she got to Carl, the harder it would be for them to avoid hitting her if they fired.

Carl showed no recognition of her or what was happening. He walked on, taking small steps, almost shuffling.

"Carl," Jas cried. A bolt flew past her, hitting the edge of the Shadow trap entrance.

She reached him and threw herself at him, pushing him to the ground. He lay beneath her, neither moving nor speaking. She looked back toward the soldiers. They were running over, the defense units bringing up the rear.

"Get away from it, ma'am," the corporal said. "We're under orders to kill all Shadows on sight."

"He isn't a Shadow," Jas exclaimed. "I told you, he's a pilot. He crashed into a trap."

"If he crashed here, where's his ship?"

"He didn't crash here. He's just come out here."

"That doesn't make any sense," said the corporal. "Look, I'm sorry. I can see the man must have been important to you. But if he came out of a trap, he's a Shadow. No question about it. Now please move away from him, ma'am. I don't want to have to make you."

Jas clung to Carl's motionless body as if her life depended on it. Her life did depend on it.

The corporal sighed. "AX7, take a hold of that woman."

"Which woman, Corporal Stormer?" the defense unit asked.

AX7? Jas remembered the designation. The unit was the one she'd worked with aboard the *Galathea*.

"The woman on the ground there," the corporal replied, irritated. "Commander Harrington."

AX7 bent down and grabbed Jas's arms. She found herself lifted gently but inexorably upright and away from Carl. As her grip on his flight suit was broken, he didn't react. He only lay there, face down in the dirt.

The corporal lifted his weapon to fire. Jas screamed, "Nooooo..." She fought with all her might, but she was no match for the metal and silicon of the unit.

The corporal hesitated. He lowered his weapon and glanced at Jas with pity in his eyes. He turned to a soldier. "Run to the vehicle and bring out the Shadow scanner, then we can show her what it is."

They all waited in silence as the sound of the soldier's running feet grew quieter and quieter. The chill wind cut through Jas's clothes, but she barely felt it. Physical discomfort was nothing compared to the agony she now faced of seeing Carl shot and killed in cold blood. He had come from the Void. He carried the trace of that place that the myth in the scanners reacted to. She was certain that the scanner would identify him as a Shadow. Kennewell stood by, pale and grave.

They all thought Jas was sick in the head, and they were humoring her. She struggled in AX7's grip, but the unit's hands were firm and unyielding around her biceps.

The soldier returned, breathless, bearing the scanner. The corporal took the device and ran it over Carl's prone form. He looked at the display. His face grim, he turned it toward Jas. She'd been correct. The display said that Carl was a Shadow.

"It's wrong," she said. "I know how this must look, but, please, you have to believe me. If you kill him, you'll be murdering an innocent man."

"AX7," the corporal said, "take Commander Harrington back to her shuttle."

He was sparing her the sight of seeing the man she loved killed.

"No," Jas shouted. "AX7, let me go." To her complete amazement, the unit's hands fell away. She dropped to the ground. She was free! The unit had obeyed her counter-command. "AX7, protect the man lying on the ground."

The unit marched over to Carl, its weapons sliding out of its arms. It turned and aimed at the corporal and his soldiers.

"AX7," the corporal yelled, "Commander Harrington has been relieved of duty. Her commands do not supersede mine."

"I obey Commander Harrington," AX7 replied.

With a gasp of frustration, Stormer lifted his weapon to shoot at Carl, but before he could fire, AX7's weapon discharged and stunned him. In response, the soldiers fired at the unit, but they were also felled by it.

In less than a second, Kennewell, Jas, and Carl were the only humans remaining conscious. The other two units hadn't moved.

"Thank krat the corporal didn't think to order them to shoot," Jas said to Kennewell, indicating the other units.

The pilot's mouth was open in an O. "Err...What just happened?"

"I'm not sure myself," Jas said. "AX7, why didn't you obey the corporal? Am I still the superior officer according to your data?"

"You are not a superior officer. You are on sick leave according to my data. But I am loyal to you, Commander Harrington. I chose to obey you."

32

Carl hadn't said a thing since Jas had rescued him from the Shadow trap. He lay on the examining bed in the *Thylacine's* sick bay as the doctor subjected him to a battery of tests. His eyes were open, but they didn't focus on anything. If food was placed in front of him, he would eat, and he would drink water that was offered. He would also stand up and walk around randomly, so the doctor kept him restrained to the bed with straps.

Jas refused to leave his side, convinced that he would be executed as a Shadow once he was out of her sight. She also kept AX7 next to her. The unit obeyed her and no one else. How it had overridden its compliance protocols, she didn't know. It was true that the defense units she'd encountered had always seemed a little more independent and individual than they were supposed to be, but this one's behavior was exceptional. She guessed that the time she'd worked with AX7 aboard the *Galathea* had made a long-lasting impression on it, and that its organic components had allowed it to develop to the extent that it could influence its programming. Whatever the reason for AX7's fidelity to her, she was grateful for it.

Pacheco requested her presence in her office, which he'd taken over, but when she wouldn't go, he was forced to come to her. His somber face appeared at the small window in the door to Carl's room. The door opened and he came in, his expression pained. He drew up a seat and sat down, hitching up his pants.

Jas was holding Carl's hand as it lay above the sheet. She looked defiantly at Pacheco.

"Jas." Pacheco rubbed his hands together as he considered his words. "I read Corporal Stormer's report, and I've spoken to Kennewell, and I'm still no wiser as to what's going on here. How about we go somewhere that we can talk about this properly? I give you my solemn assurance that nothing will happen to Pilot Lingiari."

"I'm not leaving him, Pacheco. We can talk here. I'll tell you everything, right from the beginning. And you can confirm it with Sayen Lee and the Transgalactic Council."

"All right then," he replied. "Have it your way." He told the doctor they were not to be disturbed until they were finished. He sat down again and folded his arms. "I'm listening."

It took Jas longer than an hour to tell Pacheco about what had happened at Ganymede Station, about finding myth aboard the ship—he raised his eyebrows as he heard about that—her myth run, and what the Paths had told her.

When she finally reached the end of her story, Pacheco remained doubtful. He turned his attention to Carl. The pilot's gaze was directed upward and was unfocused, as if he hadn't heard a word of Jas's story.

Pacheco shook his head. "I don't know what to make of it. What do you think the Paths meant when they said he wouldn't have a persona? Is this just his body? Is he going to stay like this forever?"

"I don't know. It's like he's in a coma, except he's awake. The doctor can't find out what's wrong with him. But he's back. That's the main thing."

Pacheco looked doubtful. "The problem is, he's officially a Shadow. That's what the scanners say. And that means that he must be rendered safe, unable to endanger anyone else. I don't know where to go from here. I'll have to take it up with the Council."

"Does Carl look like he's a danger to anyone?" Jas asked. "Talk to the Council. They'll confirm what I told you. Help me persuade them to let him go, Pacheco. Please. I just want him to be left alone. I want us to be left alone."

FOR WEEKS AFTERWARD, Jas nursed a secret hope that Carl would suddenly wake up and return to normal, but it never happened. She brought him with her to the Transgalactic Council, where she had to tell her story many more times. Supported by the testimony of the officers who had come to Ganymede Station, she managed to convince the Council that what she was saying was credible, and that Carl was some kind of anomaly—not a Shadow, but also not the person he had once been. He was a replica of the original Carl minus whatever it was that had made him himself.

But in truth Jas couldn't bring herself to believe that the real Carl didn't lurk somewhere inside the shell of his body. He'd returned from the Void looking exactly as he had when he entered it, except that his burn scars were gone. As far as she understood, the Shadows who crossed over from the Void retained the genetic makeup and the memories of their victims. She thought it was those two things that made up human personalities. If Carl had the same genes and memories as he'd had before he was taken into the Void, where was he? She couldn't understand what was missing.

Sayen stayed with her while Jas was arguing for permission to take Carl back to Earth. She was grateful for her friend's presence during the stressful negotiations, especially as she knew that Sayen was longing to see her brother again. The two women had many conversations long into the night about the Shadow War, and about Erielle, Makey, Ozment, and all the other people they'd met and some of whom they'd lost during the course of it. They also talked about what they would do when they returned home.

When Sayen left her for the night, Jas would lie down next to Carl. She would recall the days when she'd first gotten to know him. At first, she'd thought of him as just another crew member, a little awkward and flirty. She hadn't seen his kindness or loyalty or courage. Was it that she hadn't really known him then, or that he'd changed? The War had brought out a lot in people.

She felt like *she'd* changed. She hadn't realized back then at the start how alone and lonely she'd been. As time had gone on, she'd learned that she needed people. And she wasn't lonely any more. It might have looked to outsiders like she didn't have much with Carl, but that wasn't true. She had hope.

The day finally came when the Council relented and told her that Carl could return to Earth with her, providing he remained under her supervision and care for the rest of his life or until he regained a normal state of mind. She didn't need to be told twice. Within half an hour, she and Sayen were packed and waiting to leave on the next ship that would take them in the direction of Earth.

She was excited at the thought of returning to humanity's origin planet. A long time ago, all she'd wanted to do was to leave Earth. She'd looked out to the stars and dreamed of her escape. Now, with Carl, she would make it her home.

EPILOGUE

The man blinked in the bright sun. A hot breeze was blowing, drying the sweat that was forming on his skin. He was standing in the shade of tall trees, which whispered and sighed above and around him in the wind. A faint scent of eucalyptus hung in the air. He was looking out over a wide landscape of tan and brown, dry in the summer heat. The place had once been a farm, but it was overgrown after what looked like many years of neglect.

At the man's feet sat a tall woman. She had her back to him. Her knees were drawn up and her arms wrapped around them as she, too, silently regarded the desiccated view. The woman's hair was short, reddish-brown, and messy. There was something familiar about her.

Flies buzzed near the man's face and he batted them away. Though he wasn't sure where he was or what he was doing here—or even *who* he was—he wasn't alarmed. The scene around him made him feel calm and peaceful. He had a sensation that he'd been far away for a long time, but if he was patient, everything he should know would come back to him.

The man sat down at the woman's side. She turned to him with a sad smile and took his hand in hers. He remembered her name.

"Jas?"

The woman had returned her attention to the landscape, but as she heard him speak, she turned to him again, her mouth falling open. Her grip on his hand tightened. "Carl? You can talk? You know who I am?"

"Yeah," he replied. "I do." Speaking felt weirdly unfamiliar to him. Memories of the woman began to pour into his mind, and he added, "Of course I do."

Happiness welling up in him, he put his arm around her shoulders and pulled her close.

"What's been going on, Jas? How come we're back at my folks' farm?"

Her grip on his hand remained almost painfully tight. "You recognize it? You know where you are?"

"Yeah, but I don't remember coming here."

"I brought you here. Carl, you've been sick for a long time. I can't believe you're finally getting better, but you should take things slowly. Let's sit here quietly for a while and see what comes back to you, okay?"

She rested her head on his shoulder, and he sat with her, watching the still landscape under the hot sun and pale blue sky. Scenes and dialogue began to play in his mind like snatches of once-forgotten movies. The memories were jumbled and confusing at first, but the more he thought, the more shape they took, and he began to be able to slot them into order.

The recollection that his parents were dead snagged at his heart, and he bowed his head.

"How are you feeling?" Jas asked after a while. "Do you remember more now?"

"I do. It's all coming back. A few things I wish I didn't remember too."

"It's all over now, Carl. We won the war. The galaxy's at peace."

"And so after I got sick, you wanted to come back here with me?"

"I thought this was where you'd want to be."

"You were right."

Dealing with the flood of returning memories was tiring him. He lay down in the long dry grass and pulled Jas down with him. She rested her head on his chest. Above them, the afternoon sun slanted through shifting gum tree leaves.

He was silent for a long time.

"Carl?" Jas asked softly.

"Yeah?"

"What are you thinking about?"

"I'm thinking..." He took the grass stalk that he was chewing out of his mouth. "I'm thinking we should get this farm back on its feet."

He felt her nod in agreement.

Later still, he felt a patch of wetness growing wider on his shirt. "Why are you crying, Jas?"

"I'm just glad you're back."

THE END

www.ingramcontent.com/pod-product-compliance
Lightning Source LLC
Chambersburg PA
CBHW070953180726
48291CB00004B/1273